THE BOOK DOCTOR

A PSYCHOLOGICAL THRILLER

BRITNEY KING

WWW.BRITNEYKING.COM

ALSO BY BRITNEY KING

Kill, Sleep, Repeat

An intense and deadly provocative thriller which follows a woman who, in a fight for survival, realizes her job may cost more than it pays.

Room 553

Room 553 is a standalone psychological thriller. Vivid and sensual, Room 553 weaves a story of cruelty, reckless lust, and blind, bloody justice.

HER

HER is a standalone psychological thriller which covers the dark side of female relationships. But equally—it's about every relationship anyone has ever had they knew was terrible for them. It's for those of us who swam for the deep end anyway, treading water because it seemed like more fun than sitting on the sidelines. It's about the lessons learned along the way. And knowing better the next time. Or not.

The Social Affair | Book One

The Replacement Wife | Book Two

Speak of the Devil | Book Three

The New Hope Series Box Set

The New Hope Series offers gripping, twisted, furiously clever reads that demand your attention, and keep you guessing until the very end. For fans of the anti-heroine and stories told in unorthodox ways, *The New Hope Series* delivers us the perfect dark and provocative villain. The only question—who is it?

Water Under The Bridge | Book One

Dead In The Water | Book Two

Come Hell or High Water | Book Three

The Water Series Box Set

The Water Trilogy follows the shady love story of unconventional married couple—he's an assassin—she kills for fun. It has been compared to a crazier book version of Mr. and Mrs. Smith. Also, Dexter.

Bedrock | Book One

Breaking Bedrock | Book Two

Beyond Bedrock | Book Three

The Bedrock Series Box Set

The Bedrock Series features an unlikely heroine who should have known better. Turns out, she didn't. Thus she finds herself tangled in a messy, dangerous, forbidden love story and face-to-face with a madman hell-bent on revenge. The series has been compared to Fatal Attraction, Single White Female, and Basic Instinct.

Around The Bend

Around The Bend, is a heart-pounding standalone which traces the journey of a well-to-do suburban housewife, and her life as it unravels, thanks to the secrets she keeps. If she were the only one with things she wanted to keep hidden, then maybe it wouldn't have turned out so bad. But she wasn't.

Somewhere With You | Book One

Anywhere With You | Book Two

The With You Series Box Set

The With You Series at its core is a deep love story about unlikely friends who travel the world; trying to find themselves, together and apart.

Packed with drama and adventure along with a heavy dose of suspense, it has been compared to The Secret Life of Walter Mitty and Love, Rosie.

COPYRIGHT

Hot Banana Press
Cover Design by Britney King LLC
Cover Image by Britney King LLC
Photo by Ave Calvar
Copy Editing by Librum Artis Editorial Service
Proofread by Proofreading by the Page

First Edition: 2020
ISBN 13: 9798651189137

britneyking.com

For Tony, one of the finest men I've ever known

THE BOOK DOCTOR

BRITNEY KING

'Tis strange -- but true; for truth is always strange;
  Stranger than fiction; if it could be told,
How much would novels gain by the exchange!
  How differently the world would men behold!
How oft would vice and virtue places change!
  The new world would be nothing to the old,
If some Columbus of the moral seas
Would show mankind their souls' antipodes.

- George Gordon Byron (Lord Byron), *Don Juan*, Canto the
Fourteenth, Verse 101

PROLOGUE

Now

For a long time, the two of us were friends. Long being a subjective term. Long being the amount of time it takes to write a novel, and in this case, long meaning far more time than any of the parties involved preferred.

"When are you ever going to learn?" he asks, stepping in front of me. Looking me in the eye, he shakes his head. "When?"

Believe me, I wish I had an answer.

"You can't see it, can you?" It's an asinine question, considering my left eye is nearly swollen shut and the right is filled with blood. I can't see anything.

"Love is blind," he tells me—a sentiment that has everything and nothing to do with my current predicament and feels like a very good metaphor for my life up until this point.

"It's like the whole world—everyone," he says, "they all went mad."

Eventually, he ceases pontificating. He pushes me backward

into the office chair, and I tell myself, *this is it*. This is the point in which you suddenly realize the story shakes out much, much worse than you could have ever imagined.

"You know," he says, slapping the back of my head, the force of which causes blood to spray from my lips. "It really can't get much worse."

Surveying the blood that coats my desk, I beg to differ.

He spins the chair around until I good and truly can't see anything. Then he smacks me with the barrel of the gun. The crack reverberates from ear to ear, bouncing around inside my skull like a snare drum. "Write."

When I can manage and not a moment sooner, I flex my fingers. Stretch and flex. Flex and stretch. It's a scene he is used to, which is maybe why he elbows me in the face. My mouth fills with blood. I spit a broken tooth onto the keyboard. "I told you. I can't."

"You are going to die," he tells me. "Either way, you are. *How* it happens is up to you."

When he moves to strike again, I lean away. This time, I hold my hands up in surrender. I relent. "Okay…just give me a minute."

I watch in relief as he shoves the gun in the waist of his tuxedo pants. He walks toward the door and I think this is where it ends, but then, I know him better than that. With a smile, he lifts a plastic bag from the floor and raises it to eye level. "Do you know what this is?"

I'm a writer. I'm afraid I might.

He pulls out a container of lighter fluid and then another and another, counting as he tosses the empty bottles onto the floor. When the bag is empty, he drops it and fetches a book of matches from his coat pocket. On the front, the name of the restaurant where we had our first meeting. "Don't worry," he says. "It'll go quick."

My eyes dart toward the door. "Listen—"

As he watches me contemplate my next move, a grin spreads

across his face. He knows I'm thinking about what's at stake if I don't make it out of this room alive.

She will die. She will burn to death, and while he will have been the one to set the house ablaze, we both know this is a fire that started long before he struck the match.

"You see? This is what happens when a person doesn't know their own limits."

He's wrong. It's the dead of night, and even if I could manage the mile and a half it takes to reach the neighbors, it would be too late.

"You can't save everyone," he says, confirming my suspicion. "That's the problem nowadays. Everybody wants to be the hero."

He lifts me by the throat and drags me across the office. I could ask why he doesn't just put a bullet in my head and be done with it, but I don't have to. That would ruin the ending.

"It could have gone differently, you know."

I hold my breath as I crane my neck. There's a car coming up the drive. Or at least I thought there was until I discover that it's only wishful thinking. Hope will suffocate you if you let it.

My eyes flit toward the gun. His attention is on the door. That's always been his weakness, his distractibility.

He tears off a match and drags it along the rough edge of the matchbook. "I know what you're thinking…"

What I'm thinking is I've spent some time in burn units doing research. Even if I didn't love her, even if I could hate her for what she's done, I don't want her to die this way.

The match ignites. At the halfway point, he leans forward and stubs it out on my hand. I move to block him, to go for the gun, and as I do my hand grazes my face in the process. Bile rises in my throat. What was once my jawline is now just flesh hanging.

"It's okay," he says, shoving me toward the sofa. "None of it will matter when you're dead."

"You don't—"

"Now is not the time for bargaining." He strikes another

match. "Really, you should be thanking me. At least she won't have to see you like this."

My brow furrows, giving me away. I don't mean for it to happen. My poker face has a habit of betraying me where she is concerned. Automatic response is inevitable, and if distraction is his weakness, she is mine.

I'm half-seated, half-slumped on the couch when he pulls the gun from his waistband and aims it at my head. "I thought you'd be more comfortable here." He motions toward the notepad beside me. "Now write."

"You might as well just shoot me."

Before the sound of the gun firing registers, I feel the white-hot searing pain. Before I feel the white-hot searing pain, I see bone fragments fly from my kneecap. The blood makes me realize I should have made an effort.

Later, when I come to, I hear a mewling sound somewhere deep in the belly of the house. Maybe it's her. Maybe it's me. Maybe I'm dead and maybe this is hell.

He's seated cross-legged on the floor in front of me, gripping the gun in one hand, picking pieces of bone out of the carpet with the other. "The things you make me do."

I watch as he spreads the pieces of my knee out in front of him and begins fitting them together like a jigsaw puzzle. "Not bad, eh?" He flashes a smile. "What do you think?"

What I'm thinking is maybe it's impossible to survive a man like him.

"Now that you're awake," he says, "it's time to finish the story."

"I—"

"Don't. Remember? You promised."

He's right. I did promise.

That's how this started.

CHAPTER ONE

Then

Her skin is milky white, like freshly fallen snow. Her thighs are exposed. Her hair partially conceals her face. A thin dress barely covers her. One strap has fallen from her left shoulder, the other is torn. Except for the bruising, she's like a ghost, almost translucent. She is young. *How* young, I can't say. One thing is for sure—she does not look peaceful. She does not look like she is sleeping. Her eyes are wide open, glassy. Transfixed. Frightened.

Her head is shadowed by a halo of matted blood in the same shade of burgundy as the curtains in my childhood home. Knocked off balance by the memory, I stumble forward, catching myself on the curb. I'm not a stranger to the sight of a corpse. I just wasn't expecting to see one here.

Movement flashes in my peripheral vision. Glancing sideways, I see a uniformed officer taking long strides in my direction. In his left hand dangles crime scene tape.

When he reaches me, he offers a curt nod. "Can I help you?"

I realize he expects an answer, but all I can do is stare over his shoulder at the girl's face. "Sir," he says, clearing his throat. "You're going to have to move along."

"I'm—" I start to speak but can't get the words out. I swear her mouth twitches upward. I once read about "body farms" where they study decomposition, so I know it's possible. Bodies keep moving for up to a year after death. I've seen time-lapse footage. It's really quite something. Swallowing hard, I nod toward the opposite end of the lot. "I'm trying to get to the pharmacy."

He raises his hand to his brow as though to shield his eyes from the sun. He looks animatedly in the direction of the pharmacy and then back at me, stating the obvious with his body language. "Afraid that ain't gonna happen anytime soon."

Widening his stance, he partially blocks my view of the woman. When I strain and stretch upward, he follows my gaze until we're both looking at the body sprawled out on the pavement. A man stands over her, and a woman leans over his shoulder. He's taking photographs and the female detective appears to be directing the shoot.

"Wait a second..." the officer says. "I know you. You're—" He takes a step back, reaching his free hand toward his jawline and then leans forward. "You're George Dawson. Author of—"

"Yes," I say cutting him off. The average crime scene where murder is involved takes four to ten hours to clear. I don't have time for this.

He scratches his chin. "Author of those Croft books."

"No. That's Jake Patterson."

"Ah. Well, I saw the movie and—"

"Murdered?" I ask. Nodding toward the body, his eyes follow mine. Eventually, he looks back at me with mild amusement.

"It's an active investigation," he tells me. "Can't say."

"Right." I turn on my heel and start to go, but my feet might as well be cemented to the asphalt. I contemplate making a run for it. At my age, I don't think I could outrun him, but maybe if I cut out in a zig-zag pattern, maybe I can outmaneuver him.

Better not.

What I don't need is to get arrested. Or any other complications. As it is, if I don't cut out of the meeting early, there won't be enough time. Joni made it clear she can't stay. If she doesn't leave by 2:30 on the dot, she'll be late to pick up her daughter. She warned me. It can't happen again.

The other thing that can't happen again is Eve going another night without her medication. It's entirely possible one of us might not survive. "Say," the officer smiles. He shoves a notebook at my chest. "Before you go...can I get your autograph?"

He removes a pen from his pocket. "I wouldn't worry too much," he says, handing over the pen. "Probably just one less junkie on the street."

I scribble out *Jake Patterson* and head in the opposite direction.

CHAPTER TWO

'The Book Doctor'

Journal Entry

S he didn't smell bad the way they sometimes do. The way her eyes glared into mine as I fucked her...I found that pleasing, as well. Something to be said for, really. No one makes eye contact like that anymore.

Her search was endless. Whatever she was looking for—answers, a home, love, all of the above—I wanted to make sure she found it.

The lack of smell and absence of dirt under her fingernails told me she hadn't been on the streets long. That or she wasn't as bad off as the rest of them. Roaches—scattering in the daylight, but at night, well, it's a different story.

When night falls they're everywhere, which is why when I asked her where to go for a little privacy, she didn't bat an eye. "Around the corner," she pointed. "There's a parking lot."

Turns out, I should have done my goddamned homework. It wasn't just any parking lot. It was a fucking pharmacy. And do you know what pharmacies have? Cameras.

"It's okay," she said. "I do it all the time." The way she spoke made her sound younger than she looked. It made me sure she was what I was looking for: a liar.

It wasn't until after I'd paid her and rolled the condom on that she proved herself, saying, "I don't usually do this. It's actually my first time."

Obviously it wasn't true. Obviously she was trying to add to some sort of fantasy she thought I had. It worked. It turned me on — and it enraged me. I pushed her back against the wall, running my fingers across her cheek. She wasn't pretty, but she wasn't horrid either. Not like some of them. She seemed like the kind of girl who, with a little effort, might have had a shot at making something out of herself. "Do you mind if I hit you?"

She shook her head. "Just don't leave a mark."

I flashed a knowing smile and then lightly tapped her cheek. Rule number one: a little buy-in in the beginning can save you a whole lot of trouble in the end.

"Can I ask you another question?"

A slight nod.

"How many continents are there?"

She laughed nervously. "Is this a trick question?"

"Maybe."

"Good thing you're not paying me to answer questions," she said, leaning in.

Pumping into her rhythmically, at first fast and then slow, I cupped my hand over her mouth. Against her filthy ear, I whispered, "Don't scream."

She was an easy listener. Her eyes kept searching. Even in the salty glow of the dim streetlamp, I could see that they were blue with green flecks. The kind you could easily forget if you let yourself. I kept moving, eventually timing myself with the rhythm of her pulse.

When I wrapped my hands around her throat, she didn't protest. Women always put up with things way longer than they should. Maybe there's a school where they take little girls aside and teach them this, I don't know. Maybe it's the fairy tales. Whatever the case, my hands squeezing her neck...closing her airway. I'm sure she thought *this is what he's into. This is his thing. This is it. This is the money shot.*

And it was. In a different sort of way. I didn't let up, not even when she started to panic and I was forced to slam her head against the brick wall. To her credit, she didn't stop fighting, not even then. I had eighty pounds on her, easy, and a whole lot more experience. The more she fought, the harder I pressed. I squeezed and I squeezed until we both found our release. Her eyes fixed in place and blood trickled from her nose. Her breathing slowed, before it ceased altogether.

Finally, her struggle had come to an end. It was beautiful, being that for her.

"The answer is seven," I told her afterward.

For what it's worth, I let her keep the money. Not that she'll be needing it, but because it was the right thing to do.

CHAPTER THREE

The day everything changes doesn't begin particularly different than any other day. My eyes flutter open at 7:00 a.m., knowing that Joni, our housekeeper, will have left a tray with a cup of coffee that will have turned cold, along with two dry pieces of toast on my desk. After I take care of business and wash up, I will shuffle down the hall to my office, twenty-three steps away, where I will plop myself in the chair and remain hunched over my keyboard until 12:30, when I am well and hungry again.

At that time, I will take my lunch in my wife's room, next to her hospital bed, where I'll read to her what I've sweated out all morning. She'll nod, and maybe if I'm lucky, and it's a good day, I'll even earn a smile.

A smile might keep me going into the evening hours. A smile propels the story forward. They're harder to come by than they used to be, which is saying a lot. That's not to say it's ever been easy. Eve may have folded into herself, but some things remain the same. What lit her up thirty-four years ago are still the things that light her up today.

These days about an hour of me is all she can handle before her eyelids become heavy, her breathing deepens, and I hear the familiar sounds of her slumber. I try not to take it personally. She sleeps most of the time.

The doctors say it's to be expected, and I suppose it's probably for the best. "I'm sorry, darling." Our eyes meet, and for a moment she looks terrified. "I wasn't able to fill your prescription yesterday. But you'll never believe—"

I start to tell her about the body, to describe the crime scene the way I would have done in the past, before I catch myself. It's hard to know what will set her off, and I can't afford another episode like the last. Not today.

Once she's drifted off, the routine continues. I head downstairs and shuffle through the pile of mail before returning to my office to drum away some more on my work in progress.

Routine is both a blessing and a curse to any writer. You need it. Too much of it though, and the outcome is dire. Your work and your life become stunted, blurred together. Assumingly, this is how I became acquainted with the bottle.

Not that I'd call myself an alcoholic.

But that doesn't stop other people from doing it. From my agent, to my editor, to the garbage man, everyone has their opinions.

They may make alcohol the enemy, but liquor is my friend. A few drinks in, my troubles are forgotten and everything good is magnified. But that's not why I drink.

It allows me to sleep, something I haven't done much of lately. Not since things got worse.

The doorbell chimes, an alarming reminder that today is the day.

Today, the routine changes.

Joni greets our guest in her normal cheerful way, even though I've specifically asked her not to be overly friendly. Not to this visitor. Like any stray cat, if you feed them, they tend to stick around.

While I wait for Joni to show him in, I scan my inbox. Thirty-two new emails from fans await a response, plus two from my agent, and one from my editor. I comb through several emails from fans, most of which want to know when the book is coming, but the others, I leave for later, or maybe never.

It's a pressure cooker, my inbox. People are angry.

I left them with a cliffhanger and then I ended the series in what was apparently exactly the opposite way readers wanted it to go. Most people, it seems, are unaware that life doesn't always go the way you want it to.

Carefully, I ingest the latest email from my editor. The last one was a doozy. Sure, maybe I messed up by having one too many before taking on my fan mail. Maybe I was harsh, maybe I did act with a certain ferocity, but I still don't think his threats were warranted. More than thirty years of my life I've given to padding their pockets.

Between a rock and a hard place, they said they were. As though threatening legal action was supposed to soften things.

Given nothing is private anymore, believe me, I didn't come out unscathed. Some of the gems I wrote managed to make it onto social media, numerous blogs, but the worst of it...well, *it* made national news. *George Dawson Losing It?*

I'm not saying my publisher's frustration is unjustified. It was a mess to clean up, if cleaning up such a thing is possible. I write for a living. So I know better than anyone that words matter. But as I reminded my agent, bad press is better than no press.

Back then, I assumed it would all blow over. Except it didn't. Sales dropped way down. They've stayed that way. It doesn't help that I haven't released a new book in three years. Career suicide in this market, with attention spans being what they are, and consumer loyalty being practically nonexistent. It's no wonder my publisher is ready to drop me. Problem is they want to drop me *and* sue me.

In a last-ditch effort to avoid the courtroom, an agreement was reached, culminating in appearance of the man at my front door. The manuscript that was due seven months ago? Well, they want it yesterday.

My editors have assured me the man standing in my doorway, staring back at me with intense brown eyes, a sly smile, and large hands, is more than capable of managing this project. This man can apparently solve all of our problems.

He'd better.

To say that I can't afford to take on my publisher in a court of law would be a massive understatement.

"A pleasure to meet you, Mr. Dawson. I'm a big fan. *Huge.*"

"Wonderful."

Although his handshake is genuine and his smile friendly, I don't buy it. Sincerity is a virtue few in this business possess. Still, what a surprise it would be to have them send me someone who was not only an amateur but also not full of shit.

"I know the circumstances are difficult —but I can assure you—"

"These aren't circumstances, kid. This is business."

"Of course." He stares at the floor for a moment before nodding at a chair. *Eve's.* "May I?"

With a flick of my wrist, I point to the couch. "You can sit there."

We sit silently for the better part of an hour, him staring at his dreadful mobile device, me glancing over my notes. Twice he tries to engage me in conversation—I assume about why he's come— and twice I clear my throat and wave him off. Finally, dusk sweeps over the horizon outside my window, and I realize it's time for dinner. Eve is very punctual, and I don't want to keep her waiting.

I stand and motion toward the door. "That's all for today."

"It's okay," he replies without looking up. "I don't have anywhere I need to be."

"Pity."

He seems surprised by my response. Even more so when I usher him out. "I could read over your notes."

"It's supper time."

"I don't mind."

He follows me down the hall, his footsteps falling in time with mine, too close for my liking. "I do."

"Look—I know this isn't what you wanted—me being here."

I turn on my heel, and we come eye to eye. Well, almost. My shoulders hunch a little more than I'd like these days. "That's the first accurate thing you've said."

"But,"—he cocks his head—"I'm being paid to do a job and frankly, I could use the money."

"We could all use the money. That's why you're here."

"Yes, but it would be very helpful if—well…uh…you know— if we could get things sorted rather quickly."

"It's a novel. They don't just get sorted."

"No," he says. "No. I suppose they don't, do they?" He looks at me as though he's expecting something profound. When nothing comes, he fills the silence. "That's why I'm here. To help you finish the book. And…you see…I really need it to happen sooner rather than later…"

"This seems important to you," I say. Not because I really care but because it's important to find out what a person's motivations are. The sooner the better.

"It is."

"Why's that? Why not just write your own book?"

"It's complicated."

CHAPTER FOUR

He waves once and then he is gone, disappearing as easily and effortlessly as he appeared. I watch his taillights fade and I wonder, is he as glad to go as I am to see him leave? For a young man his age, it must be a relief to go back to his bustling life in the city. But if that's the case, then why was he so reluctant to go?

Standing in the driveway, the dust settles as the sound of his car fades further in the distance. I take a minute to survey the grounds, to refocus, to breathe in the evening air. Our first encounter went better than I thought, and yet, I could see it in his eyes, he is going to be a challenge.

For one, he is of the impression that he wants this. *This* being *what* exactly, I am not sure. The estate? The acclaim? The years of blood, sweat, and on many occasions, tears?

No, I doubt any of that is what he is after. Just the success. The stifling, suffocating success.

If I were a betting man—and trust me—I am, anyone who has been in this business as long as I have is no stranger to risk—I'd be willing to bet that he'll have it. He has that certain something. Something you don't find all that often. There's a quiet hunger about him, a gentle curiosity, the kind that isn't quick and flaming, the kind that won't easily burn out.

He has staying power, this Liam character, which is what keeps me in the garden long after the sun has set and a steady chill has filled the air.

His presence worries me. I am in the position to be dependent on him, which is the worst kind of position to be in. It's not a good look for me.

In fact, he worries me enough to know that change is in order.

There's something about having a visitor, after all this time, something about this particular visitor, that reminds me I'd better call the lawn guy. He hasn't come in nearly a month, maybe two. If I had to guess, I'd say his absence has something to do with his invoices going unpaid. A problem I have the power to fix. I am lazy, but not yet completely broke.

While I'm at it, I should probably look into getting a painter out, but before that, a roofer to take a look at the leak. A plumber to fix the guest bath couldn't hurt either.

This house, like all things, is beginning to show its age. With its steeply pitched gable roof, elaborate masonry chimneys, embellished doorways, groupings of windows, and decorative half-timbering, it's always felt a bit like something out of one of my novels. Dramatic, out of place, a little larger than life. Sure enough, it's a big home. Too big, if you ask me. Especially now. I told Eve that when we first looked at it. If memory serves me, I called it a monstrosity. For her, it was love at first sight. For me, it looked like trouble.

But we could afford it, and we needed more space. That was how Eve usually won: by mixing just the right amount of logic with a little emotion. I'd just signed a three book deal with Dunham, my second, and it was worth three times what the first had been. The boys were one and four, and we'd just found out a third was on the way. Eve had barely come out of what she referred to as "the fog" when the pregnancy had surprised us both

— perhaps to no one more than me, considering I'd been up at a lake rental for the better part of six months finishing a novel.

The boys were young. Caring for them was demanding and relentless. Without family around and with me writing nonstop, worried about the next novel, and with touring and whatnot, Eve had her hands in the clay by herself, so to speak.

It's yours, she said, of the baby. Of course it is. We both knew it was a lie, but once a thing like that is done, it's hard to go and take it back.

Obviously, in retrospect, it's impossible to understand what a constant reminder that thing will be once it manifests.

So, I did what I always do when it comes to Eve. I put it out of my mind. Maybe I thought I could pretend; I am a writer after all. But more than likely, I was simply too focused on work to be bothered.

That mishap, not unlike so many others, lies buried beneath the dirt in the garden.

It's one reason we're still here in this once-charming, now tired, larger than life, godforsaken house.

CHAPTER FIVE

'The Book Doctor'

Journal Entry

Consequently, I looked ridiculous. Dressed for sport, in runner's wear—it was a joke. I've only ever known one good reason to run, and that's if someone were chasing you. Thankfully, they weren't. And at least...well...at least I didn't look as ridiculous as he did.

Bent double, he was down like a sprinter, his nose inches from the humid earth. At length, he let out his breath in a long sigh and opened his eyes. Maybe he was down for the count. Maybe he was playing hot and cold.

They do this sometimes.

His jet-black hair glistened in the early morning light. I could smell the fresh scent of his shampoo. It smelled like apples.

"Get up," I said, kicking him in the ribs. Not too hard, just enough to get my point across. He curled inward, folding into himself like a wounded animal. He was dressed well, in his expensive running Lycra, and it made me smile. I wondered if he thought about it that morning as he stretched the clothing over his tanned skin. *Is this how I want to look when I die?*

I'm going to go with a negative. That's likely not what he was thinking. Men like Nick Golding only think of death in the abstract. Men like him believe they are untouchable.

As I hauled him up by his hair, I pressed the gun firmly between his shoulder blades. It was a feat, and then some, just getting him off the ground. He was not weak, at least not in this regard. Muscled and lean like a prized racing horse, he is also worth a fortune.

Not that he'll be missed. Nicky-boy was not a good man. Nothing more than a common swindler with an Ivy League education. An infuriating combination, if there ever were one. He made his fortune ripping off the vulnerable. The elderly. The incurably sick. Anyone at all, but especially anyone with no fucks left to give.

As I lead him to the edge of the cliff, he pleaded. He'd give me anything, whatever I wanted, he'd do anything. He has money.

When the bargaining failed, he moved onto the good stuff. His connections. Threats. I'd never get away with this. Do I know who he is?

Cute, this one. "Of course, Nick," I said. "Everyone knows who you are."

For just a moment, his breath switched up. It's always a bit of a blow when they find out it's not random. It's easier to accept an accident than it is the opposite.

"Jump," I told him, gripping the back of his neck the way a mother cat mouths her offspring. "Let's see if you're as good as you think you are."

"This is crazy," he stammered, trying to gain his footing.

"Would you prefer a bullet, or shall we see if you can fly?"

"Are you kidding me?"

"I do not kid."

"If I jump, I'll die." His voice came out pathetic and shaky.

"That's right."

If you really want to kill a person, it's not so hard. There are endless ways. Some quick. Some not so quick. Nick, ever the opportunist, knew that. It was such a bummer then that my options were only two. I still think of all the things I'd like to have done to him: Bind his wrists and his ankles. Take a machete and slowly peel back his scalp, carve into his brain matter, slicing little by little, peeling the meat off in layers, savoring it like you would a tender, hearty barbecue rib.

"Fine," I told him at last. "If you don't want to die…tell me… what planet is farthest from the sun?"

"Is this a joke?"

"I just told you, I don't joke."

"I don't know. Jupiter?"

An Ivy League education, to end up with this. "Jump," I said again, but he didn't budge. I could feel it. I could feel that he was running out of patience, that he was going to put up a fight. He wasn't the only one whose patience was running thin. The gun pressing at the base of his skull, I asked him once more which manner of death he preferred.

But this time, he was done talking. Nick reared back—he was trained for this, but also lazy. He swung left, as I expected him to. I went right. It took me a second, but eventually I regained control of the situation, clotheslining his skinny little neck.

As I held him over the edge, he teetered precariously. Mentally, he folded. I didn't have to see his face to know. It was an energetic conversation. His shoulders slumped and he went limp. "Go on," he said. "Shoot me."

Placing his feet on the earth, I gave him a playful shove. "You aren't worth the bullet."

He started to turn then, whether to fight or to force my hand, I

29

can't say. As his feet found only air, I watched his eyes, honing in on the way they bulged as he fell to his death.

They closed only when he hit the earth, but just for a moment, or maybe it was my imagination. When I looked down at his twisted, mangled body, his eyes were open, staring, as blue as the morning sky he faced.

My most important task for the day taken care of, my mind quickly shifted to less pressing matters. To Nick's wife at home, and his baby, a son just eight weeks old. I wondered what she'll say when the officers appear at her door. Will she fall to her knees? Or can she manage to keep it together?

Even if it was the former, she'll do okay in the end. They both will.

Maybe I'll pop by later, just to have a look. I'll lean over his crib and whisper a very important lesson, one I hope will stick with him: You have to give a person what they need, not what they think they want. I know this better than anyone.

CHAPTER SIX

Hunched over my computer, with my beverage of choice next to me, I settle in for the long haul. Tonight I have one mission and one mission only: to seek out everything there is to know about Liam Martin.

He's practically still an adolescent, so it shouldn't be too hard to dig up the kind of info I need online. I probably should have done this already, especially before allowing him into my home. But I am not that young, nor green. If I have learned anything, I have learned it's best not to cloud first impressions with things you already know.

Eve stirs in bed. The movement on the monitor catches my eye, the familiar sinking feeling in the pit of my stomach slumping my shoulders. It could be a long night. Depending.

Picking up the tumbler of Gentleman Jack, I swirl it around the glass. I take just a sip or two at first, but once she's out of bed, I down the entire thing.

She hates being down there alone, but it's safer for her to sleep downstairs. Like most lessons in my life, that one came too late and the hard way.

I am a writer and still I cannot come up with the words to

describe what it's like to have your wife, your life partner, no longer able to sleep next to you. To describe the feeling is like trying to find a word in a foreign language. It's strange and hard to grasp. Perhaps it's similar to how the French don't say I miss you: they say: *tu me manques,* which translates to you are missing from me.

The situation is what it is. I know it's safer. God, do I know. But what's safe is rarely easy. This part of her illness—the mania—and the terrors didn't come as quickly as the rest of it. And even then her episodes usually came forth in the light, so much so that by bedtime she was exhausted and slept well. But like most things, it didn't last.

I suggested moving. Eve wouldn't hear of it. This house, with its long corridors and wood-paneled walls, does not lend itself to comfort at night. It, too, seems to have a story to tell. At night, it whispers tales of the past, things we don't dare talk about in the light.

The first time Eve woke in the dark, springing to life like a feral cat, I ended up with a twisted ankle and a broken wrist. Suddenly I was not only a stranger, but an enemy. And still I didn't learn. It wasn't until the concussion that I packed her things and moved her downstairs. I'd figured she would protest, but she didn't— not even when I had to install the padlock on the door to keep her from wandering off in the middle of the night.

In that way, the Eve of today is nothing like the girl I met all those years ago.

I first laid eyes on her in English, freshman year of college. She wasn't my type at all. She was attractive, sure. But she had dark hair, whereas I prefer blondes. She was short, with the body of a gymnast, and I always imagined I'd end up with a tall, curvy type. Also, her neck was strangely long. It's an odd thing to notice about a person, but it stuck out. That's what caught my eye initially. This and she was different from the other girls. She arrived early to class and sat near the front. She took copious notes and exited the seminar with her head down, as though she were in a hurry to get somewhere.

We didn't have any other classes together, but I sat close to her whenever and wherever I could, sometimes in the library, sometimes in the dining hall. Whenever possible, I aimed for both. I admired the way her eyes crinkled at the corners when she smiled, the way she put her pencil between her teeth when she was deep in concentration. Eve may have been different, but she wasn't a loner, not like me. And I liked that. She was gregarious and charming, and she was also serious. I could sense that she swung high to low. I think a part of me needed a little of that in my life.

Toward the middle of our freshman year, as the ground began to thaw and winter slowly began to give over to spring, something shifted. It started with stories of a serial rapist. Tales began to spread around campus, and depending on who told the story, there was either a masked man exposing himself to young coeds or an even more sinister predator lurking about. A monster was grabbing young women from behind, pulling them into the bushes and doing the unthinkable.

Of course, no one actually knew anyone that this had happened to. Nonetheless, the fear around campus was palpable. Spreading like a virus, life began to change. Soon, male students were asked to accompany female students after dark. Life around campus began to look a little different.

For me, things changed for the better. This is how I actually came to know Eve. I waited for her in the library, which meant I was often the one tasked with walking her back to her dorm. She seemed annoyed by the fact that circumstances required a chaperone. But given that none of her friends hung around long into the night, nor did that pesky boyfriend of hers, she was stuck with me, and I could tell she did her best to hide her annoyance.

To my credit, I didn't try to talk to her on these walks. I did better. I listened. Sometimes, when it was just the two of us left in the library, and she was ready to pack it up and call it a night, I would make her wait, telling her I needed to get in a few more pages. "What are you concentrating so hard on over here?" she asked once, striding up to the table where I was seated.

Grabbing the paper from my hand, a devious smile spread across her face. I tried to take it back, even as her eyes deftly scanned the page. She was quick. She dodged me and ran, making it halfway across the library before I caught up with her. She wasn't laughing when I grabbed her wrist and then the paper. "What is this?"

She looked fragile, frightened maybe, at the very least caught off guard. "It's nothing."

Her brow knitted. "It's not nothing."

"It's my first novel."

"Hmmm."

I reached for it, but she held on. "Give it back."

"Say please."

"Please."

Her eyes flickered with a hint of mischief and something else. Something I couldn't yet name. "Get on your knees."

"I'm afraid we don't know each other well enough for that."

She waited for me to say more. When I stepped forward, my frame towering over her, she reluctantly handed the paper back. "You're strange."

I assumed it wasn't a compliment, so I said nothing. I turned and walked back to my seat.

"Aren't you going to ask me what I think?"

"No."

She crossed her arms over her chest. "Well, fine then. I'll tell you anyway."

"That much I assumed."

Perching herself on the edge of the table in front of me, she said, "It needs work."

I didn't look up at her. I couldn't.

"But it's not bad. It's actually really good."

"Good to know." I stared at the ink blurred on the page. She always did make me feel a little like a leaf in a hurricane.

"You know what else?"

This time I couldn't help it. My eyes met hers. "You're different."

You don't say. "You have no idea."

A wry smile spread across her face. "I like how cocky you are without even trying."

"You don't know me that well," I replied, like an invitation.

"You said it's your *first* novel. And that, George Dawson, tells me everything I need to know."

THREE NIGHTS LATER, EVE AND HER BOYFRIEND WERE STUDYING two tables over from mine. Every once in awhile she'd glance up and look over in my direction. Usually I pretended not to notice. But not then. I watched her like a challenge.

Until her boyfriend looked up, nodded my way, and made a comment that caused their entire table to erupt in laughter.

Not long after, I packed it up.

There were few things I hated more than seeing them together, and I knew the only direction it could go from there was one none of us wanted. For whatever reason—but most likely because if you imagine the worst specimen of a man possible, he would be it—he left her there in the library alone.

Eve set out, heading west toward her dorm at 12:18 a.m. By 12:23 a.m. she was attacked from behind. Her attacker drug her twelve feet until he reached a dumpster. He threw her to the ground, pinned her down, and held a knife to her throat.

She fought like hell. Meanwhile, he had trouble with the buttons on her jeans and, frustrated, he stabbed her three times. Twice in the abdomen. Eve would have bled out had she not

35

army-crawled twenty-two feet to the courtyard before passing out. By the time she was discovered at 2:27 a.m. she'd lost three-fourths of the blood in her body.

I WASN'T SURE IF I SHOULD GO AND SEE HER IN THE HOSPITAL. I only knew that I couldn't *not* go. When I arrived, her round face was the only thing visible through the sliver of glass on her door. She looked pale and tired. Like the light had gone out in her eyes. Nothing like the girl who had challenged me, holding part of my novel behind her back just a few nights before. Her parents were with her, and I could see her father pacing the floor. The boyfriend was there too.

My feet suddenly felt cemented to the floor. I could kill him for not staying. For putting her through this. For nearly getting her killed. I decided not to go in. I was only going to stay for a moment, there outside her door, just long enough to see that she was really okay. But then a nurse opened the door, and there I was, looking like a fool with my nose practically pressed to the glass.

Eve's eyes met mine, and she smiled faintly. I couldn't speak. I just stood there with a bouquet of flowers in my hand, the most expensive I could find even though I couldn't afford them. Back then, I had no idea flowers could even cost that much. But I didn't care. I've never been good with words where she is concerned. It was easier to say what I felt without them.

"You didn't have to come."

The air in the room shifted before it felt as though it had been sucked out altogether.

The nurse smiled, scooted out the door, and seemed to take any remaining oxygen with her. Eve's father looked worried as he sized me up. He looked as though every plan he'd ever had for his daughter had just flown out the window. Her mother said, "Who's this?"

"George," Eve said. She glanced over at her father. "He's my study buddy."

"The one who usually walks her home," the boyfriend said.

I balled my fists and dug my nails into my palms. I rehearsed the breathing techniques I'd read about. I counted to ten once, and then back down again. Anything to avoid punching him in the face.

I laid the flowers at Eve's side and then shuffled backward toward the door. No one said anything after that. Not until her mother suggested that she and Eve's father make a coffee run. Then it was just the three of us —and my rage—in the room.

"I'm sorry this happened," I said to Eve.

"At least they caught the bastard," the boyfriend mumbled.

"I can't have children," Eve said, looking from me to Chase or Chance or whatever his name was.

"That's the saddest thing I've ever heard."

"It's okay," she told me as she fisted the hospital blanket, eventually knotting it around her fingers until her knuckles turned white. "It's good to get your back up against the wall from time to time."

I didn't know the full extent of what that meant back then, which was probably for the best. Time has its own way of breaking us in.

CHAPTER SEVEN

L iam Martin comes back the next day and the next day and the next. We don't get much work done. Not at first. For the most part, he sits on the couch and stares at his phone while I sit at my desk, pretending to type something worth reading. What I'm actually doing is expanding upon my knowledge, continuing to learn everything I can about the man sitting across from me. He dresses funny, that much I can see. In his custom tweed suits and shiny shoes, his nice hair and stoic demeanor, he has the air of old money.

With the power of Google, I quickly become a keyboard warrior, moving onto other things that aren't as obvious. So far, I've learned about the other novels he's worked on, and the other authors he's worked with. Even if he only offered up a minimal contribution, he's good. No one is denying that.

Once I've ingested the easy stuff, I move on. Currently, I'm learning about his education, the awards he won in junior high, his stint on the debate team, as well as his starting position on the rugby team. An all-American, upper middle-class childhood by all accounts. Classic and rather boring, sadly.

This routine, my endless searches, and his endless phone

scrolling, it goes on for the better part of our first week together. A writer must obsess over all manner of things. Eventually though, he grows impatient. I'm impressed, I'll admit. I don't think I'd have been so cordial or as quiet given the same set of circumstances. But then, he's too young to know. Life goes by stunningly quick.

One day as I'm scanning through the last novel he ghost wrote, he clears his throat. "At what point can I expect that you'll show me what you're working on?"

"I have yet to decide."

"I see." He makes a clucking sound with his tongue. "In that case, can I at least trouble you for a bit of advice?"

"I can assure you, I'm the least qualified person to be handing out advice."

"Yeah, well—I'm desperate enough that that's okay."

"So you haven't heard..."

His brow furrows. "What?"

"The cheapest commodity on earth is advice."

"Please."

Suddenly, his manners make him look as desperate as he says he is. I scoot away from my desk and fold my arms, crossing them over my chest. "All right then, shoot."

He places his phone beside him and rearranges himself on the sofa, as though contemplating what it is he wants to say. "You're married, right?"

"Yes."

"I need you to help me understand women."

A belly laugh escapes. This is the most humorous and ignorant thing I've heard in a long time—and believe me, I've heard some things. "Women cannot be *understood*."

Placing his elbows on his knees, he leans forward and rests his face in his hands. "If that's true, I'm fucked."

"Aren't we all?"

After digging the heels of his palms into his eyes, he eventually glances up at me. "She got engaged," he says. "To someone else."

"I wouldn't worry too much."

His brow raises. This isn't what he expected me to say. "And why is that?"

"Half of all marriages fail."

THE NEXT DAY I'M LATE GETTING BACK FROM MY AFTERNOON WALK. After closing the gate behind me, I stop to snap a rose from the adjacent bush, a little gift for Eve. I'm headed toward the back door when something shiny in the bay window catches my eye. When I take a closer look, I'm surprised to see Eve seated at the kitchen table, her head thrown back in laughter, the familiar curve of her neck expanding out forever. She looks different, happy even. Like I've traveled back in time. At first, I think my eyes must be deceiving me. Eve hasn't left her bedroom in seven weeks. Cupping my hands against the glass, I peer in. Across from her is Liam. He's speaking animatedly, gesturing wildly with his hands. Whatever he is saying, Eve is held rapt by it.

Joni is at the sink pretending to scrub the tea kettle. I knock on the window and wave, but she's the only one who takes notice. The two of us exchange a glance.

Later, over dinner, Eve asks me to explain everything. It's a good sign. She wants the gaps in her memory filled in.

I simplify the situation, we discuss the book, the new deadline, and finally, the man who was sent to see that it happens. "So, he's like a book doctor, then," she says with a grin, and I can't recall the last time I've seen her so alive, so girlish. This comes with it, her illness, the intense highs and the very low lows. As she sticks a fork full of pasta in her mouth, I try to gauge where we are on the spectrum. You never know. One minute she might be cleaning all of the baseboards in the house with a cotton swab, and the next unable to get out of bed to brush her teeth.

She can go weeks without even looking at me.

"He's here to help me finish the book, yes," I tell her gently. It's important to tread carefully, not to cast anything her way that could be misconstrued. Nothing that could lead to feelings of guilt.

But Eve is smart. "It's been bad, I know." She slurps a wayward piece of spaghetti. "I'm sorry."

"You have nothing to be sorry for," I say, but it's one of those small lies in a marriage, the kind you're not sure why you bother keeping up with.

"I like him," she confesses. I knew that, of course. But it doesn't make it any less surprising to hear. Eve is not easily won over. Not even on an upswing. "He's interesting. He's been a lot of places. He's seen a lot."

"Has he?"

She laughs and then leans forward, placing her hand on my thigh. It's more habit than anything, but it stirs something in me. It has been awhile. "You don't know?"

"Know what?"

She peers at me through narrowed eyes, her expression equally serious and playful. She looks at me knowingly. It scares me sometimes how much you can understand the person you're sharing a life with and also not. "You haven't even bothered to get to know him."

This is truly an Eve thing to say. As though all of our problems could be solved, if only I could play nice and make friends. Lifting my whiskey, I take a swig. "He's here for work. I'm afraid we haven't had a lot of time for chit-chat."

"George," she says, a hint of warning in her voice. "Please."

"What?" I place the glass on the table and then hold my hands up, palms facing her.

"Please don't let your pride fuck this up."

THE FOLLOWING AFTERNOON, ONCE AGAIN, I FIND EVE AT THE kitchen table, Liam sitting across from her. He hasn't mentioned yesterday's conversation, nor did I ask. Stretching on my tiptoes, I crane my neck, straining to hear what they are laughing about. I must lean the wrong way too quickly because the movement causes me to pull something in my neck. I curse myself for installing double-paned windows, for aging, for allowing him here in the first place. He says something to Eve and she smiles. I can see it in her eyes. She is smitten.

That night over dinner, Eve is different. Not low, but not high, either, and I can tell we're thinking the same thing, wondering how long this is going to last. This morning, she put on makeup and curled her hair. The last time she did that was 486 days ago. I checked. It's hard to look at her. Not because I don't want to, but on account of my neck.

Joni left a bag of frozen peas out for me, to go along with my dinner. I press them against my forehead.

"How's the book coming?" Eve asks, carefully picking at her dinner salad.

I stand and shuffle around the table, taking my peas and my dinner plate to the seat opposite of her. This way I can make eye contact. "It's getting there."

Her eyelids lower, her thick, dark lashes on display. Eve does not like to be lied to. "Why won't you let him help? Isn't that what he's here for?"

"He is helping, clearly."

"George."

"What?"

"Answer the question."

"I did..." Stabbing at a piece of ribeye, I stuff it in my mouth. "Did he say that?" I ask, in between chews. "That I wasn't letting him help?"

"He didn't have to."

"Well, see…" I say, letting the fork fall onto the plate. "Then how can you know?"

"I know because he's bored out of his mind, George. And he's in love."

"So?" Sometimes Eve tries to combine two ideas that make no sense.

Now she's glaring at me like I'm the crazy one. "So. Don't you remember what it's like?"

Reaching for my spoon, I practically shove a pile of mashed potatoes into my mouth. "Hmmm."

"To be in love, George. Remember?"

Eve expects everyone around her to see what she sees. This will be no different. "What are you trying to say?"

"I'm trying to say—I've asked him to move in."

I drop the spoon and look her dead in the eye, neck pain be damned. "You what?"

"I offered him the cottage."

"Eve. You—"

"It's not like anyone's using it. He's trying to help you." She sighs heavily. "Can't you see?"

Lifting my drink to my lips, I avert my gaze. "Who said I needed help?"

"It's obvious," she says, taking the glass from my hand.

"To who? To you?" I don't mean it to be a dig, but the liquor runs warm through my veins, and I know how Eve feels about a one-sided fight.

She takes my chin in her hand and forces me to look at her. "To everyone."

Two days later, on a Monday, a breezy, early summer day, Liam Martin shows up with his belongings and moves into the cottage, 862 steps from our front door. Eve was right. It hasn't been used in awhile. She spent the better part of the weekend cleaning it out. I spent the better part of the weekend avoiding her, suddenly feeling very motivated to get this book finished and turned in.

To further complicate matters, she moved her belongings from downstairs back to our bedroom. "It'll be fine," she told me when I questioned her. "You'll see."

I didn't want to see. I knew how *seeing* usually turned out.

"Wait until you see what I've done with the cottage. You're going to love it!"

I wanted to tell her I liked it before, that it was fine as it was. But I said nothing. The cottage is mine. I had it built not long after we bought the house. Eve never much cared for it. In those days, we had more help, and I needed somewhere quiet to write, as the boys were young.

I think of Liam, how he is roughly the age that our oldest would have been, and I wonder if this is why Eve is so fascinated with him.

Liam didn't ask me if it was okay, his moving in, but I know my wife. She can be very persuasive when she wants to be.

After Joni let him in and he climbed the steps to the office, taking them two by two, he greeted me with, "Howdy neighbor."

"Funny."

"Don't worry, old man. We'll get a lot more done this way." He grinned proudly. "Just think—I'll be out of your hair before you know it."

I have no idea if he was trying to force my hand, or if for him it was mere convenience. I only know that the move was very, very clever.

CHAPTER EIGHT

I'm finishing up my normal afternoon walk, six miles, three one way and three back, when I spot him. I'm just about to round the hill when my heart sinks. The boy is a complication I don't need, not today. Tyson...or is it Jason? It's Jason, I think. Something like that.

I can't recall.

He's dirty today, as he often is, but he smiles when he sees me. Not a surprised kind of smile. He isn't shocked to see me, the way I am to see him. His smile is the familiar kind.

There's a farm up the road—a term to be used loosely—where the boy and his family live. By family, I mean there's a mom, and what you could call a dad, and maybe four or five kids. Hard to say, seeing as I try not to get too close.

He's perched on a guardrail, just off the two-lane road, staring in my direction. The closer I get, the worse it looks. His nose is runny, his cheeks are flushed, and his mess of black hair is sweaty and matted to his head. His shoes are worn through and on the wrong feet. It's unusually warm out today. Nevertheless, he's happier to see me than I am to see him. He has yet to learn what I know about life.

My mother's words ring in my ears. *Just remember, George,* she used to say, *not everyone has had the same good fortune you've had.*

"Hello," I tell him, with a slight wave. "Why dontcha come over here...back away from the road."

He looks at me almost shyly and then nods, like this is the most sensible thing he's heard all day. Sadly, it probably is.

His shirt is damp with sweat. His shorts are two sizes too small. He holds his tiny hand up toward the sun, toward me. He's eager to show off something he has found. A dandelion, I see. Satisfied by the expression on my face, he blows hard, giggling as the seeds scatter in the wind.

"Come on," I say. "Better get you home." He's walked further today than I've seen before, and this is concerning.

"How's your mom?" I ask, knowing he's too young to give me a proper answer. I'm guessing he's around three, so he can speak words. But from what I can tell, he isn't yet speaking in proper sentences. His mother is a CNA at the local nursing home, and also a waitress at the diner, and his father is a friend of the bottle.

There isn't a lot going on out here, which means word travels fast among the locals. And word has it the kid's dad is in and out of jail, mostly for domestic abuse. But also quite often for petty theft.

"Here," I say, picking him up. I sling him over my shoulders the way he likes. "Let's get there before the sun goes down, huh?"

As usual, I drop the boy at the gate. Only once, the first time, did I walk him up to the door.

I don't know what I had expected, but I don't think it was to come nose to nose with the barrel of a shotgun.

Today is only different in that his father sits on a broken-down couch, on his broken-down porch, that's barely attached to his broken-down house. He's sipping a bottle of beer, a cigarette hanging from his lips, a shotgun slung across his lap. His eyes are trained on me, waiting, wishing—hoping?—I'll cross the fence line. The boy releases my hand and starts off toward his father before turning back with a crooked smile and a salute. I wonder if his old man taught him that? Probably the only positive behavior he's taught him.

I watch him walk up onto the bowed and rotting porch and skip past his father through a half-hung screen door. I wonder if I'll see him tomorrow. I wonder what will become of him. I wonder if he'll ever make it out of here. I'd like to think so. I'd like to believe that he has a fair shot.

His father trains the gun on me and fake fires, letting the barrel float up toward the sky. He laughs maniacally, slapping his hand on his thigh, as dust flies from his filthy pants.

The boy comes out onto the porch and stares at his dad. He laughs in echo, just because it seems like the right thing to do. It's a beautiful sort of madness, thinking...or rather *believing*...that anything will ever change.

CHAPTER NINE

E ve straightens my bowtie. "You know I hate these things."
"It's good for you," she says, rolling her eyes. "You need to get out of here every now and again."

"Easy for you to say."

"Don't pout, love." She pulls tautly on my collar, adjusting the tie's position, temporarily cutting off my oxygen supply. "It doesn't suit you."

Tilting her head in one direction and then another, she checks her work. "I want you to go and have fun."

"There's nothing about this that I find fun."

"Oh, come on." Taking me by the shoulders, she turns me so that I face the mirror. "You're getting an award, not going to a funeral. Would it really kill you to show a little appreciation?"

"It might."

"It's dinner, George. A fancy dinner. I'm sure you'll manage."

"I'd manage better if you'd come along."

"I'm sorry. But I'm not feeling—"

"Your head. I know. You've said it a thousand times."

"You don't have to sound so bitter. When's the last time you had a migraine?"

I glance down at my watch. "About ninety minutes from now."

She swats at me and I duck. "I swear you act like you're eighty-nine, not fifty-nine."

"Black tie events make me feel eighty-nine."

"Just go. Act gracious. Don't complain. Then come home," she tells me with a smile. "I promise to make it worth your while."

THE CAR PICKS ME UP AT SIX SHARP. I'VE ASKED LIAM ALONG, GOD knows why, except for the fact that apparently Eve is God, because she suggested it.

I couldn't exactly say no, seeing that she said it right in front of him, and he was also invited by the Writer's Guild.

So here we are sharing the town car the coordinators sent. Here we are acting like proper friends. I guess this is why he takes the liberty to test my limits.

"I've been meaning to ask you about the boys."

Staring out the window, it never ceases to amaze me how much things can change when you aren't looking. "The who?"

"Your children."

The landscape fades into a mirage, blurred together and out of focus. My throat goes dry. Not just out of shock but also because it's been so long since those words were used in the same sentence. "I don't think that's any of your business."

"I'm sorry," he says. "You're right. I understand. It must be very difficult to talk about."

"You could never understand." I feel an anger rising in me, a sense of injustice that I haven't felt in quite some time.

"You're not the first person to know grief, George. And I hate to break it to you, but you won't be the last."

I don't answer. He's looking for a fight, and I'm not interested in competing in a suffering contest.

"It's just—" he presses. "I think maybe it would help your writing."

I imagine taking my elbow and smashing him in the face.

But then I realize that it wasn't just my imagination, because suddenly his nose is pouring blood and it's running down the front of his tux. "It's okay," he says after awhile. "I probably deserved that."

Resting my forehead against the window, I do my best to push the memories to the furthest corners of my mind.

"Eve has been telling me stories. It's been really good for her."

"Are you really telling me what you think is good for my wife?"

"You're living in a prison, George. And pretty soon its walls are going to come tumbling down around you."

"And you know all about that too, I presume."

"You'd be surprised by the things I know."

I suspect he isn't wrong about that, but there's no sense in admitting it, so I don't say anything.

"You were very successful once," he remarks, deftly changing the subject, pulling something out of my wife's bag of tricks. "I'd like that for you again. And I know, without a doubt, she wants that too. I think you owe it to her. And to your children."

I turn to him, years of pent-up rage bubbling to the surface. "You're just a punk kid who hides behind other people's work. What would you know about what anybody deserves?"

He offers an infuriating smile. "Believe me, I know enough."

THE NERVE OF THAT SMUG LITTLE BASTARD. I COULDN'T GET OUT OF that car fast enough. I was afraid if the drive lasted any longer I would have killed him. Sitting in silence in a confined space, plotting a person's death, mustering restraint you're not sure you have, is no small feat.

My first stop was the bar. I couldn't wait to have a drink. I don't remember most of the event. I only remember Liam and his goddamned popularity. Certainly, I had underestimated him. He knew everyone worth knowing and then some. By the time we took our seats, I knew that if one more person told me how *lucky* I was to be working with such talent, I was liable to cause a scene.

I've never murdered a person before, not in real life, and it's probably best not to start now, considering my advanced age.

When they call my name for the award, it takes me a second to get out of my seat, only I can't blame that on being over the hill but rather nearly under the table.

I manage to make it up to the stage unscathed despite the fact that I've had too many drinks to count. I'm pretty sure I don't even slur my words throughout the entirety of my acceptance speech. Also no small feat considering that I hadn't even rehearsed it.

I don't recall exactly what I said, except that I give some utterly charming story of how I pulled my neck pursuing a long list of honey-do's and how it's all in a day's work. Ah, the life of a writer.

The whole thing is entirely a waste of time, but everyone's either too drunk or too bored or too ready for it to be over with, and I get a very gratifying round of applause and cheering.

I'm standing at the bar afterward, feeling pretty good, thinking about everyone I've ever encountered in life. Like the waiter at the diner who was the first to learn I got a book deal. *Where is he now?*

Like the flight attendant who brought me a drink without my asking the first time I got a scathing review. *What's she up to?*

Or the lady in the airport terminal who received some very bad news by text, and everyone around her, we all stared at our shoes out of respect.

Like the publicist who I always carried a torch for, who was there when I learned I'd hit the New York Times list for the first time. She ordered champagne and told an apathetic waitress, "We're celebrating!"

Or the father I passed kneeling in the hallway of the labor and delivery wing, who would not be wheeling his wife and child out of the hospital. Did he remarry? Did he have another? Could he imagine I still think about him twenty-three years later?

It's almost too much, thinking about it now, thinking about how many significant life moments we share with people we will probably never see again. Whether we like it or not, we're all walking through life carrying snippets of each other's stories woven neatly in the fabric of who we have become.

"George Dawson."

I've just taken hold of my drink when I feel a hand on my forearm. I turn to see a striking blonde standing at my heel.

"Guilty," I say, which sounds every bit as obnoxious as it is.

"I wanted to congratulate you in person."

"Thank you."

"I'm a big fan. Well, my father was a big fan." She laughs nervously, and I find it surprising that someone so beautiful could ever feel such a thing. But then, I know women. "So I guess, in a way, that makes me a big fan too."

"Does it?"

"I've read a few of your more recent works. Although, I have to confess it's been awhile."

The bartender stares at us both as though there's nothing he hasn't heard. She leans over me. "Can I get a glass of champagne?"

The man fills a flute to the brim. The woman glances at the glass and then back at me. "Actually, make that two."

"You look familiar," I say, which is maybe the whiskey talking or maybe a little truth. It's hard to say.

The truth is she looks like Jessica Rabbit. A little overdone. But gorgeous nonetheless.

"People say I look like Heidi Klum."

I don't see it. "Ah, yes. That's it."

"I have a room upstairs…"

"I have a car waiting to take me home."

Her smile fades. "I see."

"It was nice to meet you—" I realize I haven't caught her name.

"Leslie."

"Nice to meet you—Leslie."

She presses her lips together and the smile returns. "Likewise."

"I have—"

"We have an hour yet at least before this thing ends," she interrupts. "Are you sure you won't join me upstairs for just one drink? A toast—to your success."

I don't mean to, but her suggestion makes me laugh. "There was a time in my life I might have said yes. That time has passed."

"What a shame."

"Yeah, well," I say, downing my whiskey. "Youth tends to pass you by. Whether you want it to or not."

She leans in close—not too close on account of having a champagne flute in each hand, but close enough that the warmth of her breath is hot on my ear. "You know what I say, Mr. Dawson?"

"I'm sure I can guess."

"I say we should try to hold onto our youth as long as we can. Even as it slips away, we should take hold, rebel. Refuse to let go."

"Easy for you to say. You're young. You probably don't have much to rebel against."

She cocks her head. "You'd be surprised."

And that's how I ended up in a hotel room, passed out, naked, tangled in sheets, next to a woman I didn't know.

CHAPTER TEN

I wake up after a fever dream, with cotton mouth and a sore back, the woman beside me fast asleep.

My eyes scan the room. What I wouldn't give for some cold water, a few aspirin and a time machine. I've made mistakes in my life, but not one like this, not in a long time.

Eve and I have been married for thirty-three years. Not to excuse my infidelity, but unless you've been married for that long, you don't get to have a say. You can't possibly know what an eternity it is.

For thirty of those years, I have been faithful to her.

Thirty good years. Do a couple of shaky ones negate all the good? Many people would say yes, but I don't know. I'm sure they'd be no less shaky with anyone else. That is the nature of relationships, and if I know anything at all, which isn't much, I know you can't fight nature. It always finds a way to win.

It's not like Eve's record is squeaky clean. But, like I said, thirty-three years is a long time. Days and days, hours upon hours, in which to make a mistake.

And believe me, this is a mistake. Not only am I going to have to answer to my wife for the missing hours, I'm going to have to answer to Liam, and the last thing I intend to do is to look weak in his eyes.

Bile rises in my throat. Maybe it's the pounding in my head, maybe it's the hangover, maybe it's recalling what Liam said in the car last night and how betrayed I feel by my wife. To find out that she has been talking to him about our children, when for years she has refused me the opportunity, stings.

If I were an armchair psychologist, this would be the part where I point out I've just completed a revenge fuck.

I know that Eve blames me for what happened to the boys. For years, I have known that. But to refuse me memories, pictures around the house, all of the birthdays and Christmases that I wasn't allowed to so much as mention them—well, that has been almost as bad as losing them in the first place. She made it feel like they didn't just die—they vanished, as though they'd never existed in the first place.

She blames me for them, I blame her for Jenny. I know it was hard for her, losing her brothers, and with them, in a sense, her parents as she knew them.

Most marriages don't survive the death of a child. Ours has survived three. Losing the boys sucked the joy from our lives. So much that we had none left, nothing to give our daughter. It makes sense that she rebelled. Or maybe it was in her genes all along. She wasn't my daughter. That never stopped me from loving her like she was, even when it was hard to show it. Even after the boys. Not only did I overlook Eve's mistake, I embraced it. Did I ever get credit for that? No.

I never so much as asked for it, either.

Then, when Jenny died, it took the rest of me. Not all at once, but in small chunks over the years. It was like the shedding of skin, peeling off layers of who you thought you were in the world.

I dealt with it by throwing myself into work, writing more than I ever had. Becoming more successful than I ever had. Certainly more than I'd ever dreamed. No one can tell you how much free time you have when you suddenly become childless and your wife hates you, but I can assure you, it's a lot.

I EXCUSE MYSELF FROM THE HOTEL ROOM, MAKE MY WAY DOWN TO the lobby, and end up in the hotel bar. It's not open yet, but thankfully the restaurant next door comes in clutch. I've always found the best way to deal with regret is to start over again, fresh.

The place is mostly deserted, which I find suitable. My tie is stuffed into my left pocket. It's pretty clear that I'm wearing a day-old wrinkled tux and that I haven't showered. I'm sure I look about like I feel. Experience tells me no one really cares.

A server appears to take my order. She has a large hoop through her left eyebrow and a barbell in her nose. I wonder if it hurt. I wonder if that was the point. I wonder what the next phase will be.

I order a whiskey on the rocks. Proving my point, she doesn't bat an eye at my choice. Who cares if it's not yet nine a.m.? "What I wouldn't give to have one of those," she says.

"Might as well," I tell her.

"I have an AA meeting tonight."

"Even better. Aren't those like confession, anyway?"

Her bottom lip juts out and then she nods. "Good point."

Our conversation settles my nerves. It's always been people with a kind of laissez-faire attitude who interest me most. It's as though the whole world could be falling apart and so what?

A group of businessmen eat at a corner table, laughter erupting every few minutes.

Outside, traffic grows thicker with each passing moment. Brake lights span as far as the eye can see. Horns sound cacophonously.

On the large TV in the corner, a sports channel plays. Two commentators argue in a manner that strikes me as unbelievable.

The screen flashes to a pitcher walking off the field, and that's when the unsettled feeling comes back. I look away. I hate baseball. Always have, always will.

The server delivers my drink and asks me about food. I have no appetite, but not wanting to seem pathetic or cheap, I place an order anyway. Eventually, I power on my phone and check for messages. It makes me feel sick, the weight of it in my hand, not to mention on my shoulders. I'm not a member of the generation who checks their phone every five seconds. In fact, I abhor the damned thing. If it weren't for Eve's illness, I wouldn't carry it at all.

There are seven missed calls from home and three texts from Liam.

I text back saying I'm writing and I'll be home later. This is obviously a lie, but not an implausible one. I have been known to disappear from time to time when trying to make a deadline. Of course, that was mostly in the early years when I had a bustling family life and more on my plate.

These days I'm just lazy.

Horns blare outside.

The businessmen speak in hushed tones.

Baseball goes on forever.

I wonder what it would take to get that TV shut off?

Seeing that baseball is at least half of the reason my kids are dead, I have good reason to hate it. Not that it ever stopped me before.

It wasn't *just* the sport that killed them. It was a freak accident.

Well, not so freaky, if you consider the person driving the car was at least two times past the legal limit. Although those were the words my wife used if she ever *had* to talk about it, which she rarely did. *A freak accident.*

They were on their way back from a baseball tournament when the car they were riding in ran off the road and crashed into a tree. Eve was supposed to drive them, but she was sick that weekend, and I was supposed to be the back-up.

I claimed I was sick too. Which I wasn't. I was, however, massively behind on my writing, with a deadline barreling toward me, and the last thing I wanted to do was to drive a hundred miles, round trip, and sit out in the Texas heat to watch a game I cared nothing about. I wasn't the one who signed them up. I'm pretty sure I even said that. It wouldn't kill them to miss one game. I said that too.

So when Eve mentioned that one of the other dad's said he wouldn't mind driving them, I didn't question it. It wasn't like we weren't owed the favor. Eve was constantly shuttling other people's kids here and there. She fed off of having them around. Those were the normal years. The best years of my life, although I couldn't know it at the time. And then instantly, everything was different. Everything that mattered before, those things ceased to be. Things that once seemed so pressing, turned out not to matter all that much. There will always be another deadline. And another, and one after that. Dreams don't have deadlines.

But kids die. They grow up. You grow up. You die. Bad decisions are written in permanent ink. Life cannot be reversed.

I don't realize that I'm weeping in the middle of a restaurant on a weekday. Not until the server brings me another drink, telling me it's on the house, does it occur to me that anything is amiss. People stare. Taking the glass from her hand, I salute. Liquor killed everything I've ever loved. So why shouldn't it kill me?

CHAPTER ELEVEN

'The Book Doctor'

Journal Entry

E veryone makes mistakes. Some big, some small. Depends on who you ask. Hers were big. Her biggest one would turn out to be leaving a window unlocked. Not surprising, really. Let's consider the typical American female: she can't balance a checkbook, knows all the Kardashians but not her kid's middle school teachers, can't find Iraq on a map, can't name the past six presidents, thinks the U.S. won the Vietnam War. She pays someone to mow her lawn so she can free up time to walk on a treadmill at the gym, then spends twenty minutes looking for a parking space. She waits in two lines to pay six dollars for a sixty-nine cent cup of coffee just so she can enter her office with a sixteen ounce "symbol of conformity" in her hand. She can't name her state's senators, doesn't know what a mutual fund is, has never heard of Douglas MacArthur. She spends more money on her hair and nails than retirement savings and has been brainwashed to think a man on a white horse is coming to save her.

Carefully sliding the window upward, I contemplate how a person could be so irresponsible and the many questions left to be answered. Did she not think something seemingly so small as an unlocked window could ultimately prove fatal? Was she in a hurry? How can she not see the world for what it is? Opportunistic. Evil. Every man for himself. Where was the blind spot in her thinking? How could she not see that her naiveté would put her at risk for predators like me?

In that sense, she was lucky. At least I wouldn't make her suffer. I'd make sure her death was quick and painless, even if that hardly makes for a good story.

I thought about this a lot as I waited for her to come home. Had I made the right choice? How was this story going to end? What would her face look like as she died? What was in the contents of her stomach? Did she enjoy her last meal? Or had she rushed through it, as is so often the case, mindlessly scrolling her phone?

What would be her final words? Would it be an emoji sent via text? Was that how she wanted to be remembered by the people who love her?

How many strings would she have left untied?

One thing is for sure: she was late. Her shift ended thirty-seven minutes prior. For two weeks I'd watched her, followed her, studied her. I even spoke to her once. For fourteen days, she'd come home on time. Right after work, on account of the dog. What was the hold-up I wondered? A sixth sense? Did she get caught in traffic? Had she been in an accident herself? Did she stop over for a drink with a friend?

So many possibilities. Any number of scenarios could have caused a variation in her routine. I was curious to find out how close I could come to the truth. I suppose I should've been bitter about sitting in a cramped laundry room next to the dog bowl.

On top of the washer was a basket, overflowing with dirty laundry. Clothing that would become artifacts to a loved one. Most people put them in Ziploc bags. So the smell keeps. I had a good laugh thinking of this. Grief does funny things to people. I guess I get it, but not really, I've never lost anything I really cared about. But I suppose once a scent is gone, it's gone. Who will keep hers? Her mother or father? A lover perhaps? Lucky them, her clothes stunk. A stench not soon forgotten.

While I waited, I decided to have a look around the rest of her house. It was fairly clean but sitting in that room, I realized I'd made the right selection. She was one of those closeted messy people, the kind that likes to hide things. Surely the world will be fine with one less of those.

For ninety-seven minutes I sat and I waited, stuck with B.O. and my own thoughts, which, thanks to her tardiness, weren't much better.

Then, finally, I heard the beautiful sound of a key clicking in the lock, and I knew the wait was over.

The dog greeted her at the door. A sweet dog, though useless. He wasn't a barker. Just a terrible choice she made, one among many. I wondered how long it would take someone to find her. Such a pity, the dog's bowl was empty. How long would it take before he got hungry enough to feast on her?

That I would like to see.

It took another twenty-two minutes for her to rummage through the refrigerator, microwave her findings, and flip through her phone, until finally I heard the sound of running water and I knew it was almost the end.

She looked different naked. Most women look better without clothes on, but this one, she surprised me. Maybe it was the grunge, the way she seemed ashamed of her body, wearing loose-fitting attire, as though afraid to be seen.

She was terrified, opening her eyes, seeing me standing there. Of course she was. But she was predictable in her fear, rushing to cover herself instead of going on the offensive. She bargained, too, like they all do.

Unfortunately, her fate was sealed. She liked baths, and she lived alone. She left windows open and made questionable choices in pets. She inserted herself into my story, and I inserted myself into hers.

"Listen," I said putting my finger to my mouth. "You can scream if you want. But you'll still die in the end."

She made herself small in the tub—the wrong move to make when faced with a predator. "Now, I have to ask you a question. Are you ready? It's very important."

Her eyes bulged as she gave a shaky nod.

"Who said 'Give me liberty, or give me death?'"

She looked at me like I'd lost my mind. Then her eyes darted around the small bathroom before finally landing back on me. "Bill Clinton?"

"Wrong," I said making a clucking sound with my tongue. "Would you like to try again?"

Her eyes narrowed. I could see that she was going to disappoint me...that she was going to take a guess. "Obama."

It was a mystery to me, how she couldn't answer a simple question. And, there was something else. What I'd come for. I had questions of my own. I wanted to know what true electrocution looked like. Obviously, a person shakes. Obviously, it looks like they're an epileptic having an episode. But there are other things that happen too. The body heats up, causing severe damage to internal organs. The eyeballs melt. As the body twists and gyrates, bodily functions release. The bath water turns murky brown. Skin burns off. It will have to be scraped off the sides of the tub if it is ever to be used again. That is, of course, if the dog doesn't get to it first.

CHAPTER TWELVE

To say that Eve retreats back into herself after the hotel incident would be an understatement. I have no idea how women always know when there's been someone else, but apparently, it's a superpower. No matter how many times I tell her that nothing happened, that I stayed over to write, she refuses to believe me.

Perhaps the saddest part of all is it's the truth. It was nothing. Gun to my head, I couldn't tell you one thing about that woman's body or what the sex was like. I was three sheets to the wind. If I'm going to have to pay—and it seems I am—shouldn't I at least remember what I'm paying for?

I'm a good enough writer to know a bad analogy when I see one. Obviously, the guy who killed my boys, he was probably too drunk to remember his actions. He didn't deserve to live. But he did.

And in my case, no one died. Not literally.

But Eve moves her belongings back downstairs. She stops eating, stops talking, stops doing much of anything. You don't have to be ruthless with your words if you're ruthless with your actions.

Meanwhile, I continue to spend mornings with Liam, writing, afternoons walking, and nighttime drinking myself into oblivion.

"How's it going with the girl?" I ask Liam one afternoon. Perhaps I'm desperate to talk to someone, to anyone, or perhaps I'm hoping he will bring up Eve, and in turn, my indiscretion. Most likely, I just want to hear that things are as bad for him as they are for me.

"It's not going well," he answers. "Not well at all."

"Sorry to hear it."

He looks away, out the window, before he stands and walks over to it. "My parents received a wedding invitation," he tells me, staring out at the yard. "I guess she's really going through with it."

"The sun will shine on you again."

"Speaking of—how's Eve?"

He doesn't deserve my kindness, not after the incident in the car. But then, those who live in glass houses—or how did he put it? Oh yes, *prisons*—should not throw stones. "Eve is fine."

"I haven't seen her around much."

"She's not been feeling like herself."

"No?" He turns and starts for the couch without making eye contact. "That's too bad."

I motion toward Eve's chair, then lean forward and slide it back. "Here."

Easing into the seat, he furrows his brow. I study him as he takes a pencil from his pocket, pushes it between his teeth and chews at the tip. Physically he's here, but mentally he's miles away. He plucks the pencil from his mouth. "What's the largest organ in the human body?"

Our eyes lock, and I wonder if this is a dig. Certainly it has to be. "Internal or external?"

A smile lights up his face first, and then he cocks his head as though something brilliant has just occurred to him. He retrieves a notepad from my desk and jots something down. Finally, he looks up at me. "Internal."

"The liver, why?"

"The body is such a mystery, don't you think?"

I shrug. "Speaking of—I've taken a look at your notes."

"Yeah?"

"Do you only ever work on mysteries?"

He isn't expecting the question, I don't think, which is maybe why it takes him awhile to answer. "I work on things I think will sell."

"Mysteries hardly sell anymore."

"That's not true. Who doesn't like a good whodunit?"

"What people like is sex and violence. The world is different than when I first started—back when I was your age. These days... everything has to be fast-paced. Attention spans are shot to shit. People need to be shocked out of their normal lives. And it needs to happen quick. There's no room for mystery in that."

"What's more mysterious than sex and violence?"

"I don't know—maybe I'm just jaded. I've seen too much."

He jots something else down. "How so?"

"There are only so many ways to kill and fuck."

"Ah, I don't know. I bet if we put our heads together, we can come up with something."

I lower my gaze and then swivel my chair around so that I'm facing outside. "I won't get another chance, you know."

"You don't know that for sure."

Sighing heavily, I wonder if I'm doing the right thing. "This is it for me. Which is why I'm telling you—there aren't many of us mystery writers left making an actual living. It would be prudent of you to find something else to study—something more profitable in the long-term."

"Maybe." I hear his pencil brushing the paper, scratching. "But before I give up on my dream completely, I figure I've got at least one more book in me."

I don't know whether to be annoyed or inspired. One thing is for sure, he sounds a lot like me at that age.

"Oh," he says. "And before I forget—" I swivel back around to face him. He reaches into his bag, pulls out a slip of paper, and hands it to me.

I glance down to see that I'm holding a sizable check. "I wanted to repay you guys for letting me stay in the guest cottage."

I slide it across the desk. "I don't need your money, kid."

"Just keep it. You know—for a rainy day." He flashes a grin. "Just in case we never finish this book."

———

WE WORK PAST LUNCH AND WELL INTO THE AFTERNOON. LIAM spends a lot of time scrolling, reading news articles, doing whatever he does. Every once in a while, he'll pick up his copy of the manuscript and make a couple of notes.

I write some, but not much. Mostly, I pretend to edit words, and type lines. The majority of my time I spend staring at the ink-stained pages Liam has placed in front of me.

Ever since he tried his hand at the first quarter of my manuscript, the project has gone from bad to worse. Scribble-scrabbled notes line every margin. Some of the ideas, as much as it pains me to admit, aren't half bad. And yet, I'm appalled at what he's done. So appalled that I haven't been able to make any significant progress for the better part of a week. Which is why we're sitting here in silence, him scrolling, me pecking the keyboard at a snail's pace.

All I see is red.

As the sun sinks low in the west and the sky fades to a purplish hue, I begin wrapping things up. I haven't seen Eve all day. She's been sleeping, and surely she must be up by now.

Liam clears his throat. "There's something I wanted to ask you —a favor."

Our eyes meet. I expect him to just spit it out, but of course he doesn't. "My ears are waiting."

"I was wondering if you'd mind if I had a couple of friends over. For Memorial Day." His eyes shift toward his screen and back. "To the cottage, I mean. We wouldn't bother you—or Eve."

I shrug. *What do I care?*

"Actually, I was thinking I might invite her—you know, get her out of that room."

"Eve hates parties."

"Well"—he offers me a charming grin that probably works on women but stiffens my spine—"I'm sure you could convince her."

"We'll see."

"Look, George. There's something I've been meaning to say…"

I study his tweed suit. It looks similar to one Eve bought me a long time ago. I hate suits, but I had a television interview, and neither the time nor forethought to figure out what to wear. She rescued me. She was always rescuing me. I probably wasn't as appreciative as I should have been.

"You were going to say something?" I ask as he folds his laptop, tucks it under his arm, and walks to the door.

He leans back against the frame and starts to speak but pauses long enough to stick his neck out into the hallway. He ducks in carefully, as though what he is about to say must be kept in complete confidence. "I'm sorry I brought up the children. It wasn't my place."

My stomach settles. "It's fine."

"I should have stayed with you at the hotel."

"I'm a little too old for a babysitter."

His voice low, he says, "I think Eve's angry with me."

"I don't think it's you she's angry at."

"I just want you to know—" He swallows hard before continuing, and it's then that I notice how flushed his face is. "Look, I hate conflict. But I want you to know…I don't blame you for what happened. I would have done the same thing."

"What do you mean?"

"I mean…it's only normal for a man in your position to have a fling here and there."

I have no idea what he's getting at, or how, or why he thinks this is any of his business, but he's such a good liar that I almost believe him.

CHAPTER THIRTEEN

I'm awakened by the sound of a chainsaw. At first I think I must be dreaming, but then no, there are other noises too. When the screeching grows louder, and it sounds like a freight train is about to barrel through the wall, I propel myself out of bed, flinging my body toward the noise.

At the window, it takes me a minute to get my bearings. After wiping the sleep from my eyes, I shake my head, certain that I am seeing things.

There are trucks scattered about the property, at least ten of them, some of which are on the lawn.

There are teams of people. Gardeners planting rose bushes, shrubs, workers clearing brush. Closer to the house, men are dropping paint cloths, as others tape things off and prepare to paint my house. Windows are being scrubbed, the pavement pressure washed and gutters cleared. The fountain in the garden is running and the pool sparkles like I haven't seen in a decade. As though drawn toward the window by some unseen force, my nose pressed firmly against the cool glass, I conclude, I am obviously dreaming. Then I spot Eve standing on the lawn with her hand cupped over her brow, shielding her eyes from the sun. She's smiling, and her hair is pulled up. She's dressed in something other than pajamas. It is then that Liam comes into focus. He's taking deep strides in her direction.

Snatching my robe off the bathroom hook, I manage to get it halfway on just as I bolt out of the house.

"What is going—"

"George!" Eve's face is slightly twisted. She chews at her bottom lip, the way she always does when she's perplexed. "This—"

"This is amazing!" Liam shouts over her, placing his hand on my shoulder. He gives it a good squeeze. "I can't believe it. It's like one of those makeover shows."

"This place hasn't looked this good in years," Eve laughs.

"Well done, George," Liam says. "Well done."

My eyes widen. A forklift offloads pallets of sod. "I did—"

Liam gives my shoulder another squeeze. "Everything is turning out just how you said it would." He turns to Eve. "George has been talking about this for weeks. It's all I've heard about."

I give him the side eye. "You haven't even been here for weeks."

"Ah, come on, George," he says playfully, swatting the air with his free hand, digging his fingers into my shoulder with the other. "You of all people should know you have to allow for a certain amount of creative license."

Eve looks from me to Liam and back. She doesn't know what to say.

"This is all he could talk about—how surprised you were going to be. It's been killing me not to say anything. *Killing* me. When you were so worried that he'd stayed behind at the hotel—you have no idea how hard it was not to confess what he was up to."

"We can't afford this, George," Eve says nervously. "Or we'd have done it a long time ago."

I don't say anything. I'd planned to have a painter come out and the lawn guy, but she's right. We can't afford it.

THE GET-TOGETHER LIAM ASKED ME ABOUT. WELL, IT'S NOT AT ALL what I was expecting. It's not a small affair. It's a full-blown party. The cars keep coming and coming and coming. They line the drive and spill over to the grass, where an area has been roped off. Valets take keys.

Eventually I count well over a hundred people. And that's just the ones who are scattered across my lawn. There are more by the pool and in the cottage.

It is catered, and all day, as vans arrived with flowers and whatnot, I stayed locked away in my office with little idea what was about to befall me.

"Don't worry about the cost," Liam told me. "Fixing this place up, for you guys, it's the least I can do."

At the time, I didn't know that taking the liberty to practically renovate my property would pale in comparison to the liberty he would take throwing his party.

But then night fell and guests arrived. Tents have been erected, lighting installed, a stage built for the band and an open bar. Floating candles glide on the surface of the pool.

My wife dresses up. She puts on makeup and curls her hair. She looks different than she has in a very long time.

I hide in the office, finally able to get words on the page. That is, until Liam calls up the stairs for me, which I ignore, and he finally barrels up the stairs, taking them two at a time as usual. "Come out to the garden," he says. "There's someone I'd like you to meet."

On the way down, he is distracted by a guest looking to make small talk. I scoot out the door and into the night to find Eve. Eventually, I find her sitting alone in a corner. "It's nice, isn't it?" she says, patting the seat next to her. "To have this place come to life again."

I roll up my sleeves. It's warmer out than I thought. Easing

75

into the lounge chair beside her, I exhale for what feels like the first time all day. "Is it?"

"Don't you think?"

"Only if you do."

"I want to bottle it up," she tells me, and at first I think maybe she's talking about all of the rented furniture. "This energy. This night. I want to remember it forever."

"Why? You're sitting alone in a corner."

"True," she says. "But who knows how many nights like this we have left?"

EVE HAS ALWAYS HAD A FLAIR FOR THE DRAMATIC, BUT EVEN SO, IT'S hard to discern her level of seriousness. Trying not to read too much into it, I allow myself a drink, and then another, and another, until I officially lose count.

Maybe it's the liquor, but even I have to admit the party feels magical. The scent of fresh-cut grass along with the fragrant roses, and the wafer moon overhead, it felt like a new beginning. A beginning where anything was possible, even finished manuscripts. The weekend that marks the start of summer, and with it, so much promise. "There you are," Liam says. He finds me at the bar staring up at the moon. My face turns to him, and it's the first time I notice how truly young he looks. How necessary, and how temporary.

He smiles politely. "I have someone I want you to meet," he tells me as he scoots to the side. I don't know how my expression reads, but I can only assume it isn't good. Standing in front of me, wearing a huge grin and a very short dress, is the woman from the hotel.

"This is Leslie," Liam says, placing his hand on the small of her back. He inches her forward.

She offers her hand, and, after a long beat, I take it. "A pleasure."

"It's lovely to see you again Mr. Dawson," she says doing that schoolgirl giggle thing that causes bile to rise in my throat.

"So you two have met," Liam remarks, his brow reaching upward toward the stars. "How am I not surprised? Leslie knows everyone."

CHAPTER FOURTEEN

The morning after the party, I wake early, long before the sun is up. Eve is curled into me, her forehead pressed firmly against my rib cage. I'm not sure that either of us had intended to change our sleeping arrangements, but after I'd helped her precariously take on the stairs, tipsy, we made love.

"I don't know how you can drink so much and still have your senses about you," she told me afterward.

"Who said I have any sense?" We fell asleep laughing, drunk on the possibility that it would last.

Eve sleeps in, as does Liam, or so I presume. It's Saturday, and apparently he doesn't work weekends. When he told me this, I can't say I was surprised. He's exactly the type to believe all of that work/life balance nonsense people like to spew these days.

But then he said something interesting. Something worth writing down. He said, "George, if you want to chase an elusive feeling of self-worth that you'll end up dying without claiming, be my guest. But don't expect me to. Weekends are meant for living. Isn't that what writing is about, after all? I mean...explain it to me. How can you possibly tell a good story if you don't live one?"

He had a point. I know that. I wish it were something I'd

embraced when I was his age, and I wish it were something I could swing now.

But stories don't come on a nine-to-five schedule. The muse doesn't give a shit if it's Tuesday—or if it's Saturday. The muse shows when he shows.

And this morning, he saw fit to make an appearance well before dawn on a Saturday. Luckily, I awakened with only a slight headache, not the raging hangover I expected.

Ideas popped all over the place, like the small fireworks display Liam organized last night. Not one to let a good opportunity go to waste, I grabbed a water and two aspirin and sat at my desk.

With the manuscript spread out in front of me, as my fingers moved effortlessly over the keys, I did my best to put Liam and the girl out of my mind. Every once in a while my thoughts wandered, combing through the details of last night: the girl showing up here, the party, the fireworks, Eve's naked body sweaty against mine.

This can't last; I know that. But now and again, I suppose we all want to be seduced. Even if it's not real, even though favors come with a cost. It's intoxicating.

I realize I have to nip it in the bud.

But first, coffee.

Down in the kitchen, while the coffee brews, I scramble eggs for breakfast. I've just finished buttering toast when the phone rings. My agent's name displays across the screen. Cradling the phone between my shoulder and my ear, I don't even get a proper hello in before Alan is screeching at me. "Congratulations!"

"Alan?"

"George, my friend…what the hell?"

"Good morning to you, too."

There's static on the line and already I regret taking the call. Alan is a lot to take at any hour, on any day, and maybe Liam has a point. This *is* the weekend, and it's still early yet.

As Alan complains, explaining that he tried calling three times last week, I reach for the knife, dip it into the strawberry jam, and spread it on the toast.

"George?"

Stuffing half of the piece of bread into my mouth, I mumble that I'm still here. The shower turns on upstairs.

"Your housekeeper said you weren't taking calls."

"I'm working on a book," I say when I can manage, practically swallowing the mouth full of toast down whole. Alan knows my habits when I'm writing, which means that he knows I don't take calls that aren't emergencies.

"I had to ring on a Saturday, for God's sake."

Glancing out the window, I see movement in the direction of the cottage. "As they say, no rest for the wicked."

"I guess you don't check your email, either."

Across the lawn, Liam emerges from the cottage. He steps out onto the porch, squinting into the buttery morning light. First, he surveys the grounds, and then lasers in on my house before turning his head to speak to someone inside. "I've been busy."

"Damn right you have. So I assume you haven't heard..."

"Heard what?"

"Ah, George. This is so typical of you. I don't see how you manage to stay so out of touch in this day and age."

"Hmmm."

"You hit the best sellers list."

The girl from the hotel comes out onto the porch. "Fuck."

"I know," Alan snorts. "I hate to say it—but I thought the same thing."

Jesus. I really should have fired him a long time ago. The girl inches forward, feline-like, nuzzling her cheek against Liam's chest. She's leggy and thinner than I recall. Long blonde hair, the Barbie type. Typical. It almost makes me disappointed in Liam. It certainly makes me disappointed in myself. "I don't understand."

"What's there to understand?"

Liam pulls her in close and strokes her hair. My chest tightens.

81

It could be a heart attack. It could be my sudden stroke of bad luck. "I just wasn't expecting this is all."

"So you're resurfacing. It happens every decade or so. Like fashion. You should see what the kids are wearing these days. Suddenly we're back in the 90s. Everything old is new again. Oh, and George?"

"Yeah?"

"I heard about that party of yours...brilliant!"

I can't watch my life fall apart out the window, so I make my way over to the stove and reheat the eggs. Sliding them from the pan onto the plate, the phone slips away from my ear. Alan's voice trails off. He never stops speaking. "Are you there?"

"Uh-huh."

"I heard it was mandatory your guests buy your book. I heard you auctioned them off, with tickets to your party going to the highest bidder."

"What?"

"You have no idea...man, that's—"

"I didn't—"

He raises his voice as though I'm hard of hearing, not simply distracted. "Brilliant. Really, that's brilliant."

As I fix our plates and then grab two mugs from the cupboard, Alan drones on. "Next time," he says. "Sign them. Make sure you add the date. Who knows? These parties of yours—it could be a thing."

"Right."

"Hey, George—"

I walk the plates around to the breakfast nook, which overlooks the grounds and also the cottage. Liam and the girl are facing one another, deep in conversation, deep in what appears to maybe be an argument, judging by their body language and hand gestures.

"Hello?"

The girl stands on her tippy-toes, leans in, and kisses Liam on the mouth. He says something, and they look my way. Backing away from the window, I reposition the phone. "Yeah?"

"You sound busy."

"I said that."

"Okay...well...next time you throw one of your brilliant parties, invite me, would you? I'm not exaggerating when I say I heard it was really something."

"I can't recall."

He laughs. "That's the George I know."

When I don't respond, he blows a long and heavy sigh straight into my ear. "We really need to catch up. Let's put something on the calendar. I'll have my assistant email you."

"Okay. Sure," I say, which we both know is probably a lie. Other than handing him fifteen percent of my earnings, we really don't know each other all that well, and I've never been much good at small talk.

"It's good to see you getting back in the game."

Upstairs, the shower shuts off.

"Listen," he says. "I gotta run. Tell that lovely wife of yours I say hello."

"Will do."

He gasps loudly, which causes me to wince. "Oh. Damn...I almost forgot. I read a bit of the manuscript. Have to say, it's your best work yet. Certainly better than anything that's currently on the market."

"Really?" I'm not immune to fishing for praise, especially if it's unwarranted.

"One hundred percent," he tells me. "It's going to be a smash hit. Just wait. Your fans are going to gobble this up."

"Fingers crossed." Truth is, I don't know what he's talking about. I haven't sent him anything. Which only leaves one person. Two, tops.

"Really—whatever it is you're doing—just keep it up. And don't forget...next party...I'm there. It'll be like the good old days."

Ending the call, I lay the phone on the countertop. I can't help but smile. It's nice to have him sound happy on a call. It's been a long time since such a thing has happened. Years, in fact.

Eve descends the stairs wearing a towel wrapped around her hair and a smile on her face. Something in that smile makes me think I'm going to have to find a way to keep this going, to keep Liam around. At least long enough to finish this novel, set me up on the charts, and land me a new contract.

On the other side of the lawn, the girl throws up her hands. The kissing over, it's turned into an all-out lover's quarrel, for sure. I'm glad. I've seen what women like her can do. It's like watching a fire going through dry grass with a strong wind.

"This looks amazing," Eve says, eyeing the spread. "God, George. You make me so happy."

"I couldn't ask for more," I tell her.

As Eve sips her coffee, she gazes out the window. Eventually, her eyes land on the cottage. "Liam had company stay over." She looks over at me with a sly grin. "How wonderful for him."

"Yes," I say, knowing I have to tread carefully. Some lies require more lies. This, and it has occurred to me that not only is Liam fixing my novel, he's fixing my life.

CHAPTER FIFTEEN

The girl stays at the cottage long after the party ends, long after I spy on her during breakfast Saturday morning. As a matter of fact, she stays the entire weekend, with no sign of departure anytime soon.

On Monday, during our morning writing session, Liam informs me she's had a fight with her fiancé and needs a place to hide out. He hopes I don't mind.

"It's not a good idea," I say.

"It's a fantastic idea," he assures me. "She's happy here. She said so herself."

I start to elaborate. I start to ask him to ask her to leave. In the end, I bite my tongue. Never get between someone and their desire because you will lose every time. I've been around long enough to know these things usually have a way of working themselves out.

He glances up from his phone. "You'll see." His fingers furiously text away. "I'm going to make her fall in love with me."

With a curt nod, I turn back to my writing. It's probably better not to push it. Obviously, she hasn't told Liam of our encounter, and the last thing I want to do is to force her hand. Or his.

"She's a big fan of yours, you know," he adds, proving he can't let it go. Something tells me this is a problem, where she is concerned. "In that way, you're helping me too."

"The party…it was for her wasn't it?"

He offers his signature grin. I gather Liam could have nearly any woman he wants, probably that one included, if he'd just lay off a little. I've seen the way women flock toward him, the way they swarm around. Men, too, for that matter. "It was for everyone."

"But mostly for her."

"She likes to be entertained," he shrugs. "Who doesn't want to be impressed?"

"No woman I've ever met."

He laughs in a sardonic way, matching my sentiment. "She makes me nervous. But in a good way, you know?"

"I do know."

"She makes me want to be better." He places his phone on my desk. I watch as a string of texts come in, lighting up the screen. "How did you know with your wife, that she was the one?"

"I don't know. I just did."

"I guess you can't explain love, can you?"

"No, but it never stops us from trying."

HER PRESENCE DOES MORE THAN MAKE ME NERVOUS. IT FORCES ME to look deeper into Liam's past, further into his motivations. This time, instead of a search bar, I go straight to the source, over afternoon tea.

"It occurred to me," I remark, blowing steam away from my mug, "that I really don't know anything about you."

Liam is standing in my kitchen looking out of place, like an apparition from a different time, in his tweed pants, matching vest, and crisp white button down. I've invited him to stay for tea, which I usually take with Eve, but she's down with one of her headaches again. After several beats, he looks up from his phone. "Hmmm. I'm sorry." He presses his lips together and widens his eyes. "Did you say something?"

"My wife," I repeat. "She's very fond of you. And yet, I hardly know anything."

"I'm afraid there's not a lot to know."

"I hit the best seller list." I sip my tea and try to gauge his reaction. "Surely, you knew that."

"Yes." He smiles, raising his cup. "Congratulations are in order."

"You're not just a junior level editorial assistant, are you, Liam?"

Stuffing his phone in his back pocket, he sets his cup on the counter and leans back against it. "Not just, no."

"Why are you doing this? Helping me, fixing up my house?"

"You could say I'm a fan."

"I have lots of fans—certainly not as many as I used to—but some. Surprisingly, none of them have ever repainted my home or fixed up my lawn. They never made people purchase my work in order to get into a party. At least not that I'm aware of, anyway."

"No?" He cocks his head. "That's terrible."

"You see, Liam—" I turn in my chair so that my shoulders are square with his. "I'm too old and too jaded to believe you're doing all of this out of the goodness of your heart. So, I'd really like to understand the catch—because there's always a catch. And I'd like to hear it from you."

"Straight from the horse's mouth, eh?"

"Precisely."

He pushes away from the counter and shuffles toward the kitchen sink, where he flips on the faucet. I watch as he dispenses soap into his palm and ruthlessly scrubs at his hands. "My family has money. Loads of it—too much for their own good, if you know what I mean."

"I don't know what you mean."

"But you can pretend?"

"Right."

"So, if I can help out a friend, I figure, why not?"

"We aren't friends."

He reaches for a dish towel and then turns and glances back over his shoulder. "Ouch."

IT WAS ONCE SAID TO ME THAT ANY BOOK THAT TALKS ABOUT writing is actually a book about life. It's an insult, quite frankly—to assume that one can be a great writer by applying certain principles. Truth is, it takes an immense amount of hard work over time to tell a great story.

Nonetheless, after tea, before we head back upstairs for another work session, I show Liam the library where I keep my resources on writing, countless books on craft that line the walls.

I can't recall the last time I have been inclined to pick one up. This morning, however, I was asked, last-minute, to speak at a local high school for career day, and to improve my image or whatever, my publisher said yes. I was not actually consulted, which is probably for the best, seeing that I've never been one for public appearances. But with one book on the charts and a new one coming out, my agent has assured me there's never been as good a time as now.

The talk would be unfathomable and completely off the table had they not asked Liam to stand in for me when I declined. Obviously, I couldn't let that happen, and so here we are, in the library, me looking for something to say about writing that hasn't already been said.

"If you're scared," he says, pulling a book from my shelf, "then it might be something interesting to do."

"I'm not scared. I just hate people."

"You can't hate people. Your career depends on them."

I flip through a worn book, one I haven't touched in ages, a book that Eve gave to me shortly after we were married. "I don't know so much about that."

"Writing is an act of hope, George." He glances at the book in my hand. "It assumes a future and a future reader. You know how many aspiring authors would kill to be in your position? Many of whom have the chops." He shakes his head in disgust. "Believe me, it's a lot."

"Yeah, well, anyone can cook a good dinner once."

Pressing his lips together, he starts to say something, only to seem to think better of it. Finally, he sighs wistfully. "You know the thing I love most about this job?"

I don't, but I have a feeling he is going to tell me.

"It has allowed me to understand the complexity of men. You see what's going on beneath the surface. All the things they don't say or don't talk about, those things come out when they feel they are in an environment that is safe."

"Life doesn't reward men for their vulnerability."

"Maybe not. But there's nothing so interesting as the truth."

He hands me his suggested talking points for the school. With just a quick skim, I can see that they're good. Good enough that it irritates me. "Thanks."

He reaches for the book in my hand and takes it. "I have a feeling that you and I are going to be friends, George Dawson. No matter how you try to fight it, I think you'll come to find that things just work out better with me around."

"We'll see." I snatch the book back.

Liam eyes me suspiciously but also in a way that says he isn't worried at all. Me, on the other hand, I have a bad feeling. A *familiar* bad feeling. The kind that creeps up and lingers. Helpful or not, I realize my back is against the wall. I have allowed a stranger not only into our lives but into our home. A stranger who I know little about. It doesn't make me feel any better that he seems to like being a closed book. That's the thing about mysteries—you never really think you're going to find yourself in one. But then you do.

CHAPTER SIXTEEN

Gun to my head, I don't mean to be drunk when I visit the
school. Really and truly I don't. It was Liam's idea to go to
the Italian restaurant for lunch. It was mine to order drinks.

Maybe I've had one too many. Maybe I'm just tired. Whatever
the case, for the first time in my life, I think I'm about to get on a
stage and tell the absolute truth.

Stepping up to the podium I adjust the mic to my liking,
causing it to make a painful screech. My hands shake, making it
worse, only it's not nerves. It's about three bottles of Negroni and
a salad.

"Good afternoon," I say forcefully. My voice booms
throughout the auditorium, echoing off the walls. I pull away
from the mic and tap it twice. I don't know why, other than it just
feels like the right thing to do.

The tapping causes a shrill sound to explode from the speak-
ers. Whispers grow among the audience. I clear my throat and tap
the mic once more. This time, everyone grows quiet. "They want
me to impart wisdom on you. Well, the first thing you should
know is most wisdom is bullshit—which leads me to my second

point. You should question everything. That thing that you take for granted that you're right about—question everything."

Shifting from one foot to the other and back, my eyes scan the audience. "It's just amazing to me the things the 25-year-old version of me thought—or the 45-year-old version of me thought—and I think understanding that is key. We're not very good at thinking about the things that we might be wrong about today. We're really good at knowing the ways we were wrong before. Lots of adults, we're extremely good at telling stories of how we fucked up *before*— five years ago or ten years ago, 'you should have seen me then!'—but not many of us are good about talking about today. I think that's a blind spot most people have in life, people in general. If we can apply that mindset, and say 'I was so wrong about that five years ago; I couldn't have been more wrong about that, and I know that now'... well, I think that we should apply that to the next five years, and the next ten years, and say there's a lot of shit I'm going to look back on five years from now and say 'God, I did not know what I was talking about.'"

I know my words slur, and I know I'm half-leaning on the podium as though it's an old friend propping me up. I'm a little shocked that no one gets up to stop me. But they don't. The majority of the people in the bleachers, both teachers and students alike, stare with mouths slightly open. Some of the kids are punching at their phones, but not many. Most are glued to the train wreck in front of them.

"Basically, ladies and gents...what I'm getting at is, there's a saying I've always liked: strong opinions loosely held. We should be passionate about what we're talking about—but we should leave room for questioning. You see, when you get to be a man of my age, you spend a lot of time thinking about the past, mulling over your younger days, because God knows things look better in the filtered haze of nostalgia. I like to think it's the bargaining part of the grief process. Grief, because you've accepted that you're staring at the best years of your life in the rearview mirror. I realize it's not popular thinking to tell you any of this. But the brutal truth is, we're all going to die. Some of us are closer to 'game over' than others. Few of us know how close. Terminal illness aside, age is one of the few predictors we have. So don't squander your youth thinking there's nothing left to learn. There's a lot to learn about life yet. You don't know a fraction of the things you think you do. Not for sure anyway."

I take a step forward and then back, clear my throat and go on. "There are five things you should know about writing. One: never be afraid to write about something that has had every last word written about it. It's not *your* something until *you* write about it. Two: there is nothing more interesting than the truth. Three: start with your interests. Chances are you aren't the only person on the planet with a certain palate. Four: your weaknesses are your strengths. Five: approach situations in which you feel out of your depth with sincere curiosity. Those are the handful of things I know to be true about this vocation. But there's one last thing, and perhaps the most important—activity does not make a story. *Observation* is what makes a story. How many people do you know who travel all the time but have nothing to say? Hell, I know people who went on vacation last week. They have nothing interesting to say about it. Don't be boring. Pay attention. Stories are everywhere just waiting to be found. And finally, living is making peace with the fact that you are very likely going to be the villain in someone else's story, even if you believed you were doing the right things. One of the most surprising things about life is the realization that you don't get to tell other people how to narrate their experience."

When it's time for questions, most of what is asked is par for the course. That is until one jokester stands up. "My dad says you're a hack."

"Name and address please."

The poor kid, not expecting that answer, rattles off his

personal information. Never underestimate people's capacity for stupidity. I should have added that to my speech.

"You shouldn't have done that," I say with a tsk-ing sound. "I could be a serial killer. God knows, I've written enough of them."

The boy sort of chuckles and looks around the auditorium, proud as punch. He got a reaction out of the old guy. "Relax, kid. I'm only kidding. But tell your dad when he writes a novel—or eighteen—then we can talk."

Looking out into the audience, I see that Liam and the girl are there. She has a huge grin on her face. He does not look quite so happy.

CHAPTER SEVENTEEN

'The Book Doctor'

Journal Entry

I know you shouldn't kill kids. But bear with me here— kids can be every bit as terrible as adults. Worse in fact, because life hasn't had much of a shot at hardening them. Plus, insufferable adults were once children. One has to draw the line somewhere. It's really hard to be perfect all the time, and for me, well, it's a little bit like chocolate cake. If you love chocolate cake, that is. If you crave it.

I really do.

Just like cake, when I find a kid that's worth killing, it's bliss. And I found one there that day in the auditorium. The truth is, I'd come up with a special way to kill a person, a way that I hadn't tried before, but one that I was almost certain I could get away with.

After all, how am I supposed to write it if I don't live it? Writing is about experimenting. You experiment, experiment,

experiment. Until you get it right. Until you find out what works. Murder is no different.

So I did what I did. Hopped online. Made an account posing as a pretty girl. Dug up a stock photo. Flirted a bit. Sent a few photos of someone else naked, and asked if he wanted to meet up. Of course he did.

Even though, honestly, it wasn't my best plan. I had a lot on my plate with work and all, so I figured, what the hell? It couldn't hurt to give it a go and see if he bites.

As it turns out, the idea of pussy is very attractive at that age. At any age, really. Although, before you get some sense knocked into you, well—you'll do just about anything. Especially if your IQ is a touch below average and you didn't exactly luck out in the looks department either.

The internet is a treasure trove. You can be anyone, say anything, buy anything. I didn't know exactly where to go to get what I was after, but with the few clicks of a mouse, there they were, something I didn't even know about until a few weeks ago: murder hornets.

Now, I've seen a lot of things. But I've never seen a person die by being stung to death. What an opportunity.

Murder hornets hail from Asia. Queens can grow to two inches long, which is why they're also known as Asian giant hornets.

Beyond its size, the hornet has a distinctive look, with a cartoonish and fierce face featuring teardrop eyes like Spider-Man. Orange and black stripes extend down its body like a tiger, and it has broad, wispy wings like a small dragonfly. The hornets use mandibles shaped like spiked shark fins and can wipe out a honeybee hive in a matter of hours, decapitating the bees and flying away with the thoraxes to feed their young. For larger targets, the hornet's potent venom and stinger—long enough to puncture a beekeeping suit —make for an excruciating combination that victims have likened to hot metal driving into their skin.

In Japan, they kill up to fifty people a year. Murder hornets arrived in the United States last fall. No one really knows how they got here, but I could give them a couple of clues. I ordered mine from the dark web. You'd be surprised what people keep as pets.

They didn't come cheap, but then, as they say, you get what you pay for.

The kid, whose name turns out to be Darryl, met me off an old county road just before sunset. He didn't enter the woods, but I don't blame him. I wouldn't either. He parked his souped-up sports car where I instructed him to, which should have been his first clue that something was off. No teenage girl is that thorough.

He sat in his car a while, checking his hair, tidying up, doing whatever it is kids do, before he text me, or rather Veronica, who he thought was me. He wanted to meet at his car. I agreed and told him I'd be there soon.

As luck would have it, just as I expected, he killed the engine, let his windows down, and waited.

Darryl was a big kid, bigger than I'd remembered, which is maybe why it took a little bit for the chloroform to work its magic.

The wooden box was built about six hundred feet off the road. Inside of the wooden box is a camera and a little light. It's kind of shaped like a coffin but a little bigger, a fact for which I was glad. When I had the guy build it, he asked what I wanted and I couldn't exactly say I wanted a coffin, so I said make it look like a coffin, but not. It's for a prank, I said. He could see it on YouTube; I'd send him the link, after. People do a lot of stupid stuff online, so basically after forking over two Benjamins, there were no other questions asked.

But not everything went so smoothly. For one, I regret the six hundred feet instantly. It was a real shit-show getting it out there. Even an *almost* coffin is not a small thing. Second, not only do I have to haul it 240 steps, I have to drag the kid out there as well.

Then after he's hopefully dead, I have to haul him back. All in a day's work, I suppose.

Anyway, once he was chloroformed up, I did manage to get him out to the box, and with a lot of sweat equity and a little more chloroform, I managed to get the ball gag in before stuffing him into the thing. I cut a small hole in the top on my own, just big enough to feed the hornets through and add a little handle. Then like a pumpkin, easy-peasy I placed it back on. If these things were to escape it would be very, very bad seeing as they can fly up to twenty miles an hour. They can cover long distances in no time. Who knows where they'd end up? There are a few people I like— not many, but a few—and I know a thing or two about karma.

Although, perhaps I'm getting ahead of myself.

Once the lid was on, things really started to fall into place. First, I waited for Darryl to wake up. Thankfully, it didn't take long, because the sun was about to set and I don't care for the woods at night.

He panicked a bit, which was to be expected. And yet, he too, thought it was a joke, that someone was pulling a prank on him. "You're right," I said. "Everything is a joke, and all the world's a stage. I just need you to answer a few questions for me."

It was tough getting answers out of him, and not just on account of the ball gag. Fear can have surprising effects on people. Sadly, I was worried that we'd have to do without words. "I need you to tell me how this feels. Can you do that?"

He mumbled something inaudible, which helped me know this wasn't all for nothing.

Threading the bag with the lone hornet in it, through the hole, I explained what it was. Which of course only caused more terror in poor Darryl. Lots of shrieking and flailing about like a fish ensued after that, at least as much as one can when trapped inside of a pine box.

"It's padlocked, Darryl." He seemed to calm a bit at the sound of his name. "How does it feel?"

The shrieking grew louder as he was stung. "Does it feel like having red-hot thumbtacks being driven into your flesh?"

He mumbled something else, which I can only assume was in the affirmative.

"Good," I said, before feeding the others in. "Darryl?"

There was more noise from inside the box.

"Your boxmates earned their nickname 'murder hornet' because its aggressive group attacks can expose victims to doses of toxic venom equivalent to that of a venomous snake."

Grabbing the burner phone from my back pocket, a couple of taps brought up the footage from inside the box. Not exactly award-winning cinematography, but it served its purpose.

The kid's death didn't take long. All in all, it was a bit anticlimactic, to tell the truth.

In my imagination, I had to kill the hornets, and then I had to drag the kid back to the car, drive it elsewhere, and set the scene to make it look like he died in his car, in a park. In the fantasy version, I trapped a hornet in with him for effect. The following day, I'd dispose of the box.

In reality, I just lit the whole thing up in flames and watched it —and the hornets and the body—burn. Then I just left the charred heap of disappointment in the woods. It's such a shame that reality intrudes on our good intentions. But like I said, things are hectic at work. Sometimes good enough has to be good enough, and there's one less disrespectful teenager running around, so we should all be glad for that.

I did expend some effort moving the car to a second location. No point letting a giant red flag stay that close to the crime scene.

Even so, the most disappointing thing, aside from knowing I could have done better, was the lack of the media reports about the murder hornets, the ensuing frenzy, and the inkling of satisfaction that I caused it.

CHAPTER EIGHTEEN

I can't shake this terrible feeling, apparently not even from my dreams. The foggy haze of sleep settles, refusing to immediately lift just because consciousness is trying to make an appearance. Pulling myself from sleep to the surface feels like trying to pull myself from a well with a rope. My head feels like it weighs ten thousand pounds, my eyelids equally heavy. Sleep beckons me backward, like waves, knocking my sharp edges off.

I ask myself what I know, running through the events of the day in my mind. It started out as normal. I hadn't meant to fall asleep. A fine summer's morning, one that had turned out better than I'd expected. Joni made her famous strawberry and spinach salad with honey balsamic vinaigrette for lunch, which Eve and I ate outside by the pool. Afterward, Eve had taken a swim, and I sat in the lounge chair jotting notes about the book. While progress has been made, there's only a few weeks left until the deadline, and I'm not close enough.

Liam and I had a productive morning session before he retired back to the cottage, telling me he was taking the afternoon off to run into town.

When Eve finished her swim, she suggested we head upstairs

for a nap, which I assumed correctly was code for sex. That's what we used to say when the kids were young and we wanted to get a quickie in. It brought back memories of summers past, in a good way.

After we made love, I powered up my laptop and brought it to bed as Eve slept beside me. At some point, I must have dozed off, because when I wake, I am slumped forward in bed, pillows propped behind me, drool coming from my mouth. Glancing over at the clock, I try to remember what time it was when I fell asleep. That's when I hear Eve's voice calling and I realize she isn't in bed beside me. Pulling myself completely upright, it hits me—the sweet, musky, unmistakable smell of smoke. My mind races to the children. Maybe it's the post-nap fog, or the two whiskey sours I had after lunch, or maybe it's just that the parent in you never dies, even if children do, but I have the overwhelming sensation of needing to get to them.

Leaping from the bed, I bound down the stairs, taking them two at a time. The smoke is worse on the first floor, blindingly thick and suffocating, like someone has opened my mouth and shoved a hot piece of coal straight down my throat and into my lungs.

Like a cannon, my chest pushes outward in rapid deliberate bursts. "Eve!"

She calls for me again, and my feet propel me in the direction of her voice. Smoke has filled the hallway. Its thick, black haze overpowers my senses. Finally, I reach Eve in the kitchen. "I warned you, George. So many times I've warned you," she says.

It's not the first time she's used these words. They're familiar, reserved for *special* occasions. Usually when I let my guard down. "Why don't you ever listen?" Her eyes are fixed on the floor, never wavering. "Why do you make me do these things?" This is Eve's troubled voice, throaty and devoid of emotion, the one I do my best to avoid.

As I round the counter, I laser in on what's causing the smoke.

Flames billow from a frying pan on the stove. A container of vegetable oil sits beside it, empty.

Flipping the burner off, my eyes scan the room in search of a lid. I check the cabinets, but they're all gone. I rifle through the kitchen looking for baking soda and find nothing.

Removing my shirt, I wrap it around my face and bolt toward the laundry room, where I keep a spare fire extinguisher hidden. Eve has removed the one that belongs in the kitchen.

The fire alarm flashes through my mind. I wonder why it hasn't gone off. Looking up at the ceiling, it becomes clear. My wife has ripped it from its socket. No doubt she'll have done the same to the others. It wouldn't be the first time.

This is why we can't have nice things.

"You really shouldn't have done that," she says when I return with the extinguisher in my hands. After I put out the grease fire, I look down at her. Those eyes, there's so much history in them, but it's not there now. What's reflected back to me is not the Eve I know, it is not the woman I married, it is not the mother of my children.

She's seated on the kitchen floor, sprawled out, her legs splayed in front of her. A knife lies on the floor between them. Across her lap is the shotgun that is supposed to be locked in a gun safe in my closet. Eve doesn't know the combination, or so I thought. But it's not the shotgun that worries me most. It's what is in her left hand. A hammer.

"Please," I say calmly. There's so much more to be said, but the rest of it won't come and doesn't matter. "Don't do this, Eve."

'This is all your fault," she tells me with spit flying from her mouth. She's full of rage, possessed, past the point of rationalization. "You don't love me, George. You never did."

"That's not true," I say, glancing toward the door, glancing at the shotgun, thinking about what's at stake if I don't get this situation under control. Carefully, I go over to the sink and fill a glass with water and gulp it down. Eve rests the hammer across her knee and picks up the knife.

I look in the direction of the driveway. "Joni go home for the day?"

She glares at me. We both know the answer. My attention turns to the cottage, and I try to discern whether Liam's there, whether he would help or harm the situation, whether putting him in danger would be worth it.

"I lied, you know."

"Yes."

"And ever since, you haven't loved me."

"I've always loved you."

"You can't love a liar."

She's taken that line from my manuscript, I realize. I shouldn't be surprised she's read it, but I am. "You're sick, Eve. There's a difference."

"I'm going to kill you, George. I'm sorry, but I have to."

"No, you're going to drink this water," I say as I squat next to the safe under the sink and quickly punch in the code. I retrieve Eve's medication, holding it up for her to see. "And you're going to take these pills and then you're going to rest."

"Maybe," she says. "But first I'm going to kill you."

EVE DOESN'T KILL ME. NOT IN THE PHYSICAL SENSE. SHE AIMS THE gun at my chest, dead center, but forgets to chamber a round. It takes a bit of a fight, but eventually I pry it from her hands. The knife is on the floor at our feet, and in the scuffle I graze the blade, slicing into the arch of my foot. Blood smears the tile like abstract art, when all is said and done.

While I'm handling the gun, she goes for the hammer. She manages to get a few swings in, first ravaging my back, and a good one to my right shoulder. Covering my head, I push my body into hers, pinning her against the wall. I need to keep her from being able to swing.

Annoyed, or tired, or both, she drops the hammer. As it lands on my toe, Eve begins pummeling me with her hands. She beats her fists into my chest and then scratches at my face before she moves onto my hair. She grabs a fistful as I do my best to restrain her.

I have learned over the years, it's easiest to let her get out what she can during the initial assault. Otherwise there will be a second round, which comes exactly around the time you think it's all over.

It's never all over, but that isn't the point.

Taking her to the ground and pinning her there, I have to be careful. Eve, while fierce, is also tiny, and it would be easy to hurt her. One thing I cannot afford is a hospital visit. For me or for her, but especially for her, because I am an expert at explaining my injuries away, whereas Eve, more than once, in a state of mania, blamed her injuries on me. She may have multiple diagnoses, but the law is the law. Due process and a proper investigation have to take place, regardless of my wife's mental health status.

Kneeling over her, my knees press her arms into the floor, holding her in position as I weigh my options. Her head swings from side to side, wickedly, as she screams at the top of her lungs. I cup my hand over her mouth, but it barely muffles the sound and just enrages her, adding fuel to the fire.

I could run from the house, but if left to her own devices, there's a good chance she would harm herself or our home. As it is, I'm lucky to have woken up when I did. And even if I could escape her, where would I go? What would I come home to?

Finally, the writhing from side to side subsides and the screams quiet. It's like a toddler throwing a tantrum—Eve has to wear herself out. I weigh my options. The wrong word or the wrong choice can send her right back into a fit.

"You're hurting me," she cries. "Get off!"

"I'm keeping you safe."

"I'm not safe," she hisses. "Nothing with you is safe."

I remove my left knee from her arm, easing up on the weight I'm putting on her. This allows her to swiftly reach up and backhand me, busting my lip in the process. "I hate you!" She spits in my face.

That does it. I lift her from the ground, grabbing her at the elbow, and drag her out of the kitchen, through the living room, past the library, and down the hall to her room downstairs.

She puts up a fight, but her second wind is no match for mine. Deftly, I push her up against the wall and place my hand at her throat, my fingers holding her chin in place. "Do you want them to put you back in that place?" I scream, spittle coating her face. Not only am I angry, I'm hurt. And I'm tired. "Because if you want to kill me, that's how you do it."

She glares at me through widened eyes as though I'm the crazy one.

"I don't know what I'm going to do with you," I say. "For fuck's sake, Eve, you almost burned the house down. How many times are you going to do this before it ends up being the last?" I'm yelling in her face, years of white-hot anger spilling over.

Tears spring to her eyes, but that means nothing. When Eve is in this dark of a place, nothing gets through to her.

I shake my head slowly, careful to exaggerate my movements. I need the message to sink in, even if I know deep down it won't. "We have to get you help."

Eve's knees buckle and she slowly slides to the floor. The mania takes a toll on her. When she starts to come down, it often happens quickly.

Her expression has morphed from a cornered animal to concern, her eyes softening and welling with tears. When she looks at me this way, it's hard to believe what just happened. It's as though she is seeing me for the very first time. "You're going to send me back there, aren't you?"

"I'm not sending you anywhere—"

She starts to weep—full-on sobs.

"It's just...we need more doctors. The medication isn't working anymore."

"If only you didn't have to make me so angry."

I look down the hall toward the front of the house and then back at my wife. "What is it now?"

The sobbing stops just as quickly as it started. "You know I hate parties."

CHAPTER NINETEEN

I'm betting that the cut to the center of my foot is not a clean one. Under normal circumstances, there is no doubt this would warrant a trip to the ER. But with Eve locked in that room, and our houseguest God knows where, I don't want to chance leaving her alone. That, and it's my driving foot. Even if I could manage, it is one more variable I don't need.

I take a deep breath in and hold it. Then I peel back the dish towel to take a peek at the damage.

Instantly I wish I hadn't.

I can see bone. Trying to assess the depth, I poke around a little bit. The flesh looks like raw meat, red and angry. Unfortunately, I was right: it's a jagged cut. Eve likes to go for the bread knives. With six attempted suicides under her belt, she's hardly a novice.

They were supposed to be locked away and hidden, but I'm guessing she managed to sneak one past Joni yesterday as she prepared lunch.

It's not so bad, I tell myself, opening and closing the slit down the center of my foot. I pull the skin together taut, until it meets and hold it in place. I'll just grab my fishing kit, down a couple of drinks, and hope for the best. With a little luck, it'll turn out like any other night.

After rewrapping my foot and securing the bandage in place, I hobble around the counter and flip on the monitor in Eve's room. She walks in circles, fingers trailing the walls. When she reaches the door, she presses her ear to it and then jiggles the handle. Obviously, she knows it's locked. Still, there is defeat written on her face.

As I survey the mess, I comb the cabinets in search of the alcohol. I'm going to have to clean the wound and wrap it, temporarily, before stitching it up, just until I can get this place cleaned and restored to normal. Once the drinks start, anything goes, and the last thing I want is for Joni to walk into this tomorrow morning. She's seen a few things in her time, for sure, but nothing to this extent.

THE FOLLOWING MORNING THE DOORBELL RINGS EARLY. EARLY enough that Joni hasn't arrived, early enough that I haven't even made it out of bed, much less downstairs. Liam's car is parked in front of the cottage. He got back late; it was nearly 1:00 a.m. when his headlights pulled through the gate. I was still scrubbing the kitchen.

I can't imagine he'd be coming over to borrow milk at this hour, nor is his work ethic favorable to such an early start, which is how I come to the conclusion that it isn't him.

I'm not expecting anyone in particular, but I'm surely not expecting to open my front door to see uniformed officers staring back at me. *Good God, what now?*

They look like Harry and Moe from *The Three Stooges*. The scene would be almost comical if it weren't so early and I weren't as hung over as I am. I can see on their faces that I am not what they were expecting either.

"Morning, Mr. Dawson," the shorter of the two says. He leans forward and balances on his toes before falling back on his heels.

Pulling my robe around me tightly, I tie it in place. I'm sore all over, like I've been hit by a freight train as opposed to my five foot two inch wife. I'd hardly managed to pull the robe around my shoulders when I swung the door open. Aside from it being haphazardly thrown over me, I'm shirtless and in boxer briefs. My hair stands on end, and my busted lip is caked in dry blood. If the officers take offense to my appearance, they're good at not showing it. "We wanted to speak with you about a boy who has gone missing."

"Goddamn it," I say, looking past them, over their shoulders, out at the road. My mind flits to the kid with the dandelion. To his crooked smile and broken-down home. "Is he dead?"

The two exchange a glance.

"Why do you ask?"

I shake my head. "I just assumed that's why you're here."

"Well, actually, we were hoping any information you can provide might help us determine his whereabouts."

I should have done something when I had the chance. I shouldn't have taken the kid back there. "Have you checked with his father?"

"We have. He shared with us that the boy had been upset over something you said."

"Huh?"

"His father said there was some sort of misunderstanding...a joke or something that was made when you gave a talk at his school?"

Rubbing at my temples, I exhale. He continues. "His parents said he seemed to perk up not long after the incident. Other than that—"

"Other witnesses," the tall cop pipes in, "have confirmed that you warned him he should be careful. Something about serial killers and whatnot." He turns and looks around the yard. He clears this throat before turning back to me. "His father said the boy threatened to pay you a visit, he was *that* bothered."

"Really?" I swallow hard. *This is the last thing I need right now.* I say a dozen Hail Marys and then silently pray that I'm still fast asleep in my bed upstairs and that this is all a dream. It's the only thing that comes close to making any sense. In front of me stand two cops inquiring about a missing kid. And here I am assuming I know who they are talking about, because it would take both my hands to count the number of times I've found him on the highway and have taken him home, only to realize we aren't even talking about the same kid.

The short guy looks at me all funny-like. "Mind if we come in?"

"Actually, yes." I glance over my shoulder. "My wife is still asleep and, as you can see, I'm not dressed."

The tall one fishes a card from his pocket. "Give me a call. We can set up a better time to chat."

With a nod, I take the card from his hand. I've written enough crime fiction to know better than to say anything more than what has to be said.

CHAPTER TWENTY

I deliver Eve's breakfast to her room: two dry pieces of toast and a protein bar. It's probably not the breakfast of champions, but I don't have much more in me. I doubt she'll eat it anyhow.

As I unlock the door and enter the room, she doesn't stir. Sleeping in the fetal position, her dark hair matted around her head, she snores quietly. She almost looks peaceful. Better not to wake her.

Softly I place the plate at her bedside and tiptoe toward the door. It reminds me of when the kids were young and would fall asleep in the car. I'd carry them to their beds, stealthily making my way down the hallway and into their rooms, moving heaven and earth, silently, praying they wouldn't wake.

It's like this now as I decide to let Joni give Eve her meds later, making it clear that I can't have Eve out of her room. Not today.

Today I need to focus. My deadline is barreling down, speeding at me like a bullet train. On top of this I need to put in a call to Eve's physician. And while I'm at it, I need to find some time to consider my predicament. If they don't find the kid from the school, my life is about to become a little more unpredictable.

I shove the sedatives into my pocket, pull the covers up around Eve's shoulders, and lock her back in. Afterward, I retreat to my bedroom to shower, and by the time I have finished, Joni has arrived.

Joining her in the kitchen, where I have cleaned the blood and reorganized everything that was upended in the struggle, we both notice that the smoke still lingers. We both sense that something is off.

"Burned dinner last night," I say as she peers at me over her thick- framed glasses.

She cocks her head letting me know she doesn't buy it. "I left the casserole in the fridge."

"Felt like eating something else," I say. "Fried chicken."

She presses her lips together and then nods. She never comments on my personal life. She doesn't have to. "How's Eve?"

Opening the refrigerator, I peer into the abyss. "Rough night."

"I can stay late," she replies. "If you need me to. My daughter is with her father."

"That would be nice." After grabbing a bottle of water, I go over and stand at the window. Liam is making his way up the drive toward the back door. I glance back over my shoulder. "Oh, and Joni—"

She's scrubbing at a grease stain on the stove I must have missed. She looks up. "Can you make sure Eve takes these just as soon as she's up?"

Joni looks down at the horse pills I have placed in her hand and then back up at me. "Sure thing."

LIAM ARRIVES LATE FOR WORK. HE SITS ON THE COUCH ACROSS from my desk and sulks. Aside from the sulking, even though I attempt conversation, he's quiet and not his usual self. When I ask him about his trip into town, he finally spills the beans. He tells me the girl left. She went back to her fiancé.

I don't have the heart to tell him they usually do. He's droning on: he's not sure if he wants to stay here any longer; it's terrible being out in the cottage all alone; he hates sleeping by himself. "You can't imagine what it's like," he says, although he has to know I can. "This is severe emotional pain."

"It will pass."

He looks at me like I've lost my mind. "It took every ounce of will in me to get out of the bed and walk over here. You have no idea."

I give him a look that assures him I do. But I don't say much. Mostly because he doesn't let me get a word in edgewise. "If I'm not in love I cannot be happy."

"You're one— maybe two—one night stands away from feeling better. Promise." I tell him this, even though deep down I know it is not essentially true.

"You can have all the pussy in the world, George, and still not be happy," he retorts, looking affronted.

"I bet most young men your age—hell, even the old ones, for that matter—would beg to differ."

"You know what it's like being in my apartment in the city, in that cottage, to hear footsteps echoing down the hall and no one there? The spot in the bed next to you empty? Who could possibly be happy in a situation like that?"

A lot of people stuck in unhappy marriages, I almost say. I keep my mouth shut because I know it won't help, and I understand his point. Finally, I just shrug.

"I don't know what I did wrong."

"Love doesn't care about right and wrong," I say. "Love is blind."

He looks over at me with exhaustion written across his face and the kind of blanketed pain that tells me we're never going to finish this book. "What am I going to do?" More than once, he sighs heavily. "How can I fix this?"

Seeing how broken-up he is, how close to the deadline we are, I tell him the truth. "If you want her, you have to trap her."

"What?"

God, this kid, he has so much to learn. He's smart, but not nearly as smart as he thinks he is. "Why do you think we have so many animals hanging out in zoos?"

"I don't know." He shrugs. "Because they make money?"

"We tell ourselves these animals cannot survive in the wild, but that's a bit far-fetched, don't you think? They're animals, and instincts are very powerful."

"Yeah," he says, and I can see he doesn't get it. "But how can you make someone love you, if they don't?"

"You can make a person believe anything, Liam. After all, you're a writer, aren't you?"

AFTER LUNCH, WHICH I EAT WITH LIAM IN THE FORMAL DINING room, he asks if I'd like to work outside on the balcony for a bit. It's been a few days since I've felt the sun, and I could use a change of scenery. Fresh air will do us both some good.

He brings along a small notepad, he paces the length of the space, stopping every once in a while to jot something down. He appears to feel better after our talk, which is good, because it meant he actually got some work done. At one point, he writes a beautiful line, proving grief can, in fact, be profitable. *My heart still has her fingerprints on it, should she ever change her mind.*

"George?" He stops pacing and stares in my direction of the cottage.

"Yeah."

"You asked me why I don't write my own book. Remember?"

Our eyes meet. "Yes."

"They won't give me a book deal," he says. "That's why."

"It takes time. You'll get there."

"You ever play sports?"

I shake my head. "Never."

"Well, hopefully you'll follow this analogy anyway." He stuffs the notepad and pencil in his pocket and then gestures wildly with his hands. "Let's say you play soccer and you're great at defense. They say it's your strong left foot. But you know you'd be really great as a forward just the same. Only because there's no one better than you that can step up on defense, you don't have a chance in hell at moving up the field."

"Okay?"

"That's why I haven't written my own book."

"Perhaps," I say, "you should stop being so damned good on the defensive end."

Later that afternoon, we're wrapping things up, when on his way out, Liam stops inside the doorframe and turns back. His brow pinches together. "What happened to your face?"

"We've been together all day and you're just now asking me that?"

"I was waiting for you to tell me."

"You'll have to keep waiting, I'm afraid."

He looks partly amused and partly like he doesn't really care one way or another. "Where's Eve?"

"She's not feeling well."

"I see..." He shuffles from one foot to the other. "Maybe I could talk to her—you know, cheer her up."

"Maybe," I lie. "By the way," I say, scooting out from my desk. "Remember that kid at the school?"

"Which one?

"From my talk...the smartass."

He shakes his head. "You're going to have to be more specific. There were a lot of smartasses. They're teenagers, George."

"The one who stood up and said I was a hack."

"Oh, sure..." His eyes narrow. "I think."

Now that I can see for sure that he is lying, I glance back at my screen and add the item to my cart. For less than fifty bucks, I am about to become the proud owner of a Mobile-200 GPS tracker. The reviews look great—"A great tracker for cars and assets!"— not that I put too much weight into those.

Nevertheless, according to the specs, it should serve the purpose for what I need. It appears easy enough to use and most importantly it touts a long battery life. Two to three weeks between charges. I should be rid of him by then. And I can track him straight from my dreaded phone, receiving real-time alerts if the tracker enters or exits an area, with updates to its location every thirty seconds.

The toughest part will be finding the time to install the damn thing to the underside of his car, but I'm sure I can think of something.

I could kick myself for letting Eve allow him to stay here—for not paying more attention to his comings and goings. I suppose I was too preoccupied with my own.

"Earth to George—hello?" When I look up I can see that he is annoyed. Liam doesn't like people who start things they don't finish. "What about him?"

"He's missing."

"Oh." He rubs at his chin as though the truth has just come to him. "Wait—the one you told you might be a serial killer and that he should watch his back? That kid?"

"I didn't say that last part."

His eyes don't blink for forty seconds. At least. "Are you sure? You'd had a lot to drink."

"I'm sure. I checked the video. See for yourself. It's all over the internet."

"Fuck."

"Yeah." I one-click the tracker. "Anyway, the cops came by.

They'll probably want to talk to you, seeing as how you were there with me."

"No problem." He sighs. "You've got my number."

CHAPTER TWENTY-ONE

'The Book Doctor'

Journal Entry

I wasn't ready for another, but everything happened so fast. When you love something, you don't have to have a reason to do that thing. You enjoy it. It becomes second nature. Plain and simple. Like I said before, it's like cake.

But sometimes, even if you enjoy it, it doesn't mean it's always convenient. Most things people love rarely fit neatly in the confines of their lives. More often than not, they have to make them fit.

It's possible this isn't making any sense. Stick with me. It's not easy describing your desires to another. People make a real mess of it. At any rate, I'll do my best.

Let's say, other than cake, you really, really like deep dish pizza. Picture it—the kind with the gooey cheese that oozes, stringing out, adorning your fingers as you attempt to shove it in your mouth. The kind with the perfect crust and the sauce that bubbles on top. Now, imagine the best you've ever had.

If you really, *really* like pizza, as I do, it's obvious that you'd enjoy it from time to time. Same with cake, but it's more socially acceptable to pig out on pizza. It's a meal versus a dessert. But everyone knows too much of a good thing quickly becomes a bad thing. Sustenance can be risky if you're not careful—as evidenced by the extra inches that tend to creep up around your gut after you've indulged.

More than likely, it would do you well to go for a salad, but if a pizza is calling your name, and it's something you love, it's really difficult to abstain over the long haul. And sometimes you just have to have it, for no other reason than you simply cannot get it out of your mind.

That's what killing is like. Sometimes I can't *not* do it. It's like a craving— it's a void that has to be filled. Other times it's merely the path of least resistance, something that needs to be done in order to take care of business and get on with the rest of my life.

This was one of those times.

Bobby Simmons lived in a nice house, though too big for just one person, if you ask me. A waste, but then, that pretty much sums him up.

It was dark out, a moonless sky buried in the clouds. It was hot and muggy. Restless kind of weather. The kind that makes you want to do terrible things.

Unfortunately, he had an alarm system. One of those fancy kinds, the kind that are not easily disabled. He was a paranoid fuck, through and through.

Gated, closed off, buttoned up, just like the owner, his house was practically a fortress. I know. I'd been given the grand tour. The panic room I did not see with my own two eyes. I heard about it secondhand.

Beside his bed rested a 9 mm and a dog that is essentially a pony, trained to attack on command. That's the kind of guy he was. What she saw in him, I have no idea.

Preferably, if I had the time or the initiative, I wouldn't have handled it like I did. I would have thoroughly enjoyed breaking and entering, sedating a small horse, and force-feeding pills down a man's throat.

Alas, sometimes shortcuts are the way to go. Sometimes any pizza will do because you just want pizza. The end result will be the same. He knew a thing or two about that. She didn't love him, anyhow. If she had, she wouldn't have been sleeping with Nick Golding, cliff-jumper extraordinaire. Nor would she have been sleeping with me. His death will no doubt send her running back.

Ideally, I wouldn't kill two people who can be tied together, but then, life doesn't always work out the way you want it to. Personally, I blame six degrees of separation. I assure you, it makes it pretty hard. Harder still if the woman you're in love with has a sex addiction and fucks anything that breathes.

But, like the weather, it is what it is.

At 5:02 a.m. on the dot, Bobby Simmons exited his front gate, headed east with his one hundred and eighty pound, four-legged running mate. I did not set out on foot. I remained in the comfort of my vehicle. Letting him get a running start, I watched the clock, counting down the minutes until my life improved.

At 5:04, I put the car into drive. By 5:05, I'd run him down. In the rearview mirror, he looked like I'd imagined, perfectly splayed out on the pavement, lifeless. Meanwhile, man's best friend sniffed the roses in a neighboring yard.

CHAPTER TWENTY-TWO

Liam shows up for work the following morning whistling—I assume on account of the girl. If only I were feeling so chipper. The sound of his engine had me up a little before four this morning. It was sometime after six when he returned, emerging from his car with coffee and bagels. He brought them over with him when he came. His haul included several everything bagels, complete with cream cheese. Eve's favorite. It makes me wonder how he could know this about her. How much has she told him?

She was up and about this morning and seems slightly more herself. Maybe the bagels helped. Whatever it is, I'm glad for the improvement. I could use a bit of a reprieve. It's crunch time on the manuscript, and I'm going to have to make a run into town to pick up her medicine.

Her doctor advised me to ease off the sedatives a little, which I don't have a choice on, considering I'm running low and he's hesitant to refill the prescription without seeing her in his office. It would be a nightmare to get her there in this state. She's been hardly coherent. And quite frankly, I don't have the time to spare.

Unfortunately, mental illness does not care about deadlines or careers, or fitting into a neat little block on a calendar.

Instead, the doctor has another medication in mind that he thinks might help. It's a new drug, but if it keeps Eve from killing herself or burning down the house, I'm game.

"What does she do in that room all day?" Liam asks, catching me off guard, pulling me back to the here and now.

"She watches her programs."

"Programs?"

Sometimes I forget his age. "Her TV shows."

"All day?"

"She has a schedule," I say, which is the truth. What I don't say is that she stares at the TV catatonically and most of the time, when she's in a low place, cannot recount a single detail about what she's seen.

His bottom lip juts out. "That's wild."

"After lunch," I tell him, "I'm going to have to take a break and run into town."

"Mind if I join you?"

I scan my inbox. I wonder if he'd like to handle my fan mail. There are hundreds of new emails; I simply cannot keep up. "It's fine."

"You don't look like you're going anywhere very fast with your foot that way."

"I managed a walk around the grounds yesterday, didn't I?"

He scoffs. "A very, very slow one."

"I recall you having to jog to catch up."

"Suit yourself," he tells me. "But if you change your mind, we can take my car."

My car is fast. But it's not as fast, nor as new, as Liam's. I don't particularly fancy myself to be the kind of man who is distracted by shiny things. But I'm a man, nonetheless. And I envy that car. This, and, I'd rather not leave him here alone with my wife.

THE SUN REFLECTS OFF THE PAVEMENT IN HAZY WAVES. EVEN before noon it has turned out to be a stifling hot day. "You want to drive?" Liam asks, pretending to toss his keys in my direction.

"Better not," I answer with a nod toward my foot. As I slowly make my way around the Audi, I reflect that Liam is right, I probably wouldn't get far if left to my own devices. My foot is noticeably sorer than it was yesterday. Stopping to breathe into the pain, I notice a long scratch and a large dent on the passenger side of the car. Liam notices me looking, concern written on his face.

"You gonna make it?"

"Yeah," I say, bracing myself against the hood of the car. "What happened?"

"Hit a deer the other day." He shakes his head from side to side. "Bastard darted right out in front of me."

When I don't say anything he waves a hand in the air, "Ah well, you know. That's what insurance is for."

Once we get out on the road, it's easy to see how Liam could damage his car. He's a terrible driver. Not only is he reckless, he appears to have zero qualms about getting us killed.

"Slow down!" I shout. He has the top down, music blaring. It takes me repeating myself twice and slugging him in the shoulder before he hears me.

Squinting, I think I see something up ahead. Although, because Liam is driving like a bat out of hell, whatever I thought I saw is suddenly behind us, fading fast in the passenger side mirror. "Turn around," I tell him, waving my hands.

He turns the music down. "Huh?"

"Turn the car around," I say at the top of my lungs.

He slows and then does a spin, going far too fast. When the car is facing the opposite direction, he laughs and says, "You mean like that?"

He's a goddamned child. If he doesn't crash the car, I may die of a heart attack.

"What are we doing?" He stares at me quizzically. "Did you forget your wallet?"

I point. "Slowly," I say. "Take it about twenty. Then two hundred yards that-a-way stop."

He does as I ask, coming to a slow stop not far from the boy who is sitting on the side of the road, squatted down in the grass.

"There," I say to Liam. "That's what we're doing."

His eyes shift. "What the fuck? That's a kid."

Opening the door, I extend my hand. The boy is hesitant. He doesn't know me in this context. He's used to seeing me on foot. He backs away. "Come on," I wave. "It's me, George."

He doesn't budge. "You want to go home?"

To my surprise, he shakes his head. I can't blame him. I don't want to go there either. Liam holds out a bottle of Tic Tacs. He shakes some into my palm. I offer them to the boy. His little hand reaches out from the brush. I start to refuse him, to tell him to get in the car and then he can have them, but I think better of it at the last second. I'm sure he's scared enough as it is. At the same time, I know I can't walk him home. Not with my foot in this condition.

"Ask him if he wants ice cream," Liam says with a nudge.

"Have you got any ice cream?" I ask, glancing around the interior of the car, intending to look as ridiculous as he sounds.

"No. I don't know...I've seen it in the movies. Isn't that how you get kids in the car?"

"How should I know?"

His brow knits together. "I just assumed this isn't the first time you've found him on the side of the road."

Liam is good at making a point. "I don't think we should take him home right away. Let's make his parents sweat it out."

"I have a better idea. Let's take him to the police station and tell the cops we found a lost kid."

"Ah," Liam says. "Irony."

I shrug.

He peers out the passenger door and then looks at me, his face impassive. "First, we have to get him in the car."

"Hey kid," I say. "You want to go get ice cream?"

CHAPTER TWENTY-THREE

The boy babbles in the back seat, and I don't know why, but it physically hurts. I haven't been around children much since my own were little. That's sort of the thing about having kids—once you no longer do, unless your vocation has to do with teaching, there aren't a lot of opportunities to be around them, even if you wanted to. Especially as a man.

I think about my children a lot. Where would they be now, what would they be like? I think about how they would essentially be different people, all grown up, not very much at all like the kids I knew.

With Jenny it was different. She was older when she died, and I got a bit of a glimpse into what adulthood with her would have been like.

Jennifer was Eve's daughter through and through. She not only inherited her mother's looks, she inherited her mental illness too. The boys' deaths were unexpected, like curve balls, to use a familiar expression. But Jenny's was different. It was slower to evolve. Most people that kill themselves don't succeed on the first try, and Jenny was no exception.

We spent nearly $100,000 on facilities and treatments, trying to make her better. Like Eve, she would improve for a while. But never for long. Her manic periods were always extreme. Maybe this had to do with the fact that she was a female adolescent. I don't know. But Jenny's rough patches were never pretty. Jenny wasn't a particularly happy child before the boys died, but she was *never* happy afterward.

I resented her, of course. I resented her for not being mine, for not appreciating the life I was trying to give her. I resented the fact that she was alive and miserable, when her brothers did not get the chance to be either of those things.

So when she told me she was going to take her own life that final time, when she said that she'd find a way to get the pills, or the knife or the rope, I didn't try to stop her. I didn't put her in her seventh consecutive facility. I didn't listen to Eve, who said we should.

I knew Jenny was right. It's impossible to keep every item that a person might use to kill themselves out of reach forever. I just hadn't thought it would happen like it did.

THERE'S A SMALL TOWN IN BETWEEN WHERE WE LIVE AND THE CITY. Hamilton has three restaurants, several fast food joints, a small grocery store, a bank, a pharmacy, and of course, a bar. Normally, I use the pharmacy in the city on account that some of Eve's medications require compounding—and also the privacy it allows. Everyone knows everyone out here, and people talk. There's not much else to do.

I wasn't looking forward to the long drive on account of work, about two and a half hours round-trip, give or take traffic, nor did I want to leave Eve alone for that long. So I'm not entirely upset to have found the boy. Even though we need the medication, postponing the trip into the city is not the worst thing that could have happened.

The boy speaks gibberish, pointing out the window as we pass the old hardware store. It closed up a few months ago after old man Stott died. His kids had moved on to bigger and better things, to live their lives elsewhere, and without anyone to run it, it dried up.

The bank has changed hands several times, but it keeps going, as banks have a way of doing.

Next to the bank is the drugstore. It's an old-school pharmacy, the kind with a soda fountain that serves root beer floats, banana splits, milkshakes, and ice cream of all kinds. By the early 1920s, almost every drugstore had a soda fountain. Due to prohibition, which began in 1919, bars were closing and people needed a place to socialize. This place was born of that time.

"It's rather charming, don't you think?" Liam says, glancing at the boy in the rearview mirror as he pulls into a parking spot up front. "Almost makes me think maybe I could live out here in the boonies."

We used to bring the kids here when they were little. Sometimes in the evenings, Eve would make me promise, after a long day, that I'd drive them into town to get root beer floats. She'd bribe them with it to keep them out of her hair. I don't think I appreciated her enough back then, what she did, raising them, tending to their needs and mine too.

I suppose it's tough to see things as they are when we're in the thick of it. All I know is that my career was demanding, it was all-consuming and in hindsight I can see that there wasn't enough of me left over for her, or for them.

Inside the shop we grab ice cream. "Lovely family," Mrs. Thompson remarks as the boy spins round and round on the barstool. She's feeble, and her memory is half gone, but she shows up to work every day, and I suppose that's what keeps her going.

Nevertheless, it strikes me that under different circumstances, she could be right. I could be doing this very thing with my son and grandson. A long time ago, I did research for a novel about parallel universes, and while I don't know if they exist, I'd like to think there are other versions of Eve and I out there somewhere, happy with our children. Children who are alive. Children who are having children of their own. In some ways it's easy to imagine. In others it feels very far away. The part of me who existed as a father then is not in the same place as the person I am now. His growth was stunted when life as he knew it was cut off.

I send Liam next door to the dime store to buy the kid a new pair of shoes. The boy devours the ice cream, so I buy him a cheeseburger and fries. He eats all of it and half of mine too.

Later, when we take him home, his old man is passed out on the porch drunk. He stirs at the sound of Liam's tires crunching on the gravel road.

"Let me deal with this," Liam says, as I reach for the door handle.

Through the windshield I watch as Liam walks the kid up to the porch, even though I warn him not to. I have a feeling this is a very bad idea. Next thing I know, the hood of Liam's car is riddled with bullet holes.

CHAPTER TWENTY-FOUR

'The Book Doctor'

Journal Entry

He was a filthy bastard, that's for sure. A rotten heap of human waste. A kink in the chain of existence. It's an anomaly that he'd made it this long, but somehow he had. Lucky me.

First, I parked outside the bar and waited. While I waited, I had a lot of time for research, a lot of time to inscribe the pages of this journal. So much time.

He was a last call kind of guy, which was no big shocker. It was better for me, anyhow. If he was nice and drunk, there wouldn't be a lot of fight left in him. Even so, it was surprising what he could do. Rednecks are built that way. They're certainly tougher than they look. This I found out the hard way.

A half hour before closing time, I punctured the rear tire on the passenger side of his truck. In the dark, I doubted he'd notice. I was also betting even once he realized he had a flat, that he'd be drunk enough to make the dumb move of trying to make it home. It's not easy to change a tire when you're properly sloshed.

I should have known this wouldn't deter him. He wasn't the brightest of the bunch. I came upon him crouched over his tire, surveying the situation. It felt like sweet karma, considering the damage I'd seen him inflict.

I'd imagined clubbing him with his own tire iron. But there's a saying about the best laid plans, and I know better than to marry one scenario; this is a broad universe with infinite possibilities, even when it comes to hillbillies.

We had a bit of a tussle, the two of us. Once an understanding was reached and he was well tasered, I made sure to tie him up tight. Snug as a bug in a rug, as my mother used to say. After wrapping him up all cocoon-like, I stuffed several old socks in his mouth and wound duct tape around and around his head. Then I took him, swaddled sweetly in his cocoon, and I got a long rope. I attached the rope to the cocoon, which I hooked onto a makeshift trailer hitch I'd jimmy-rigged onto my sports car.

It wasn't ideal, but I knew it would suffice.

Once he was adequately secured, I drove him up and down the country road his kid likes to wander. I varied the speed, slow at first and then fast, so I could be sure he felt it.

I wondered what he'd look like when all was said and done. Would his body even be recognizable?

The breeze blew through my hair as I rode ever closer into the future with the top down. It was a beautiful night, warm and windy. Bright stars littered the sky, while his body parts littered the ground.

As I stared at the center line and thought of all the things I had yet to do in the world, all the lives left to save, I thought about how irresponsible he was and how someday his son would thank me for what I'd done, even though he'd never know it was me. You can do a lot of good in this world, if you don't care who gets the credit. I wondered if the boy and I would ever be in the same place, like serendipity, if our paths would ever cross again. I pictured myself in Paris, maybe London, or some small, middle of nowhere town. Maybe I'd go out for a stroll, and we'd pass on the street. I'd look at him and nod hello. Such a simple gesture, and yet, it would mean so much more than either of us will ever know.

CHAPTER TWENTY-FIVE

First it was the headline in the paper about the hit and run. Then things started to hit close to home. Too close to home. They'd found Jon Monroe's truck out off County Road 249. I hadn't known that was his name, had I? It's funny how you can memorize a person's face, but not their name. Innumerable details there are to sort out in life.

The story goes that Jon Monroe went out one night for a drink and never came home. It's a familiar tale, and one that wouldn't be out of the ordinary for him.

Had it not been for the truck, no one would have thought much of it. I've known a bender a time or two myself. I certainly wouldn't have questioned his absence.

If it hadn't been for all of the blood splattered along the pavement, the police might not have even taken a second look. Men like Monroe don't often make headlines for turning up missing. His photo will not draw the kind of attention that causes command centers to be erected or volunteers to rally. Not many folks around here will be eager to form search parties or to spend their time putting up flyers. Men like Jon Monroe are rarely missed.

But aside from the blood, it was the rest of the story that drew people's attention. The lack of a body. Limbs and other body parts had been strewn about, spanning a range of more than a mile and a half. A hand here, and a foot there, the rest of him nowhere to be found. It makes for a rather peculiar situation, the kind that gets people talking. Had the rest of his body been trapped and drug under a vehicle, and if so, where had it ended up?

I didn't think much of it, other than what would become of the boy and his mother. Not even when I tuned into the news and saw the clip about the hit-and-run in Austin did it occur to me that something was off. I hadn't considered that the two crimes might be related. I'm a writer. I'm proficient at seeing connections, and also in making them up where there aren't any, which means I have to be careful. Plus, I had other things on my mind.

Still, I told myself I'd look at the tracker, just to see. Liam had come in late a few nights before, hadn't he? And there was the dent in his car.

He certainly had motive to kill the boy's father, considering that Monroe had peppered his car with bullet holes. I'd seen the look in his eyes, the contained but eerie manner in which he'd restrained himself afterward.

Although it wasn't that which told me for sure he was involved. It wasn't until I saw the girl on TV pleading with the public for someone to come forward in her fiancé's death that I understood what I was up against. It wasn't until she showed up at my doorstep, devastated, looking for Liam, that I knew with certainty; this situation is much more than I bargained for, and I am in deep, deep shit.

CHAPTER TWENTY-SIX

I have my attorney contact the sheriff's office about the missing kid from the school. He has told me what I already know: unless they can prove that I'm somehow involved with his disappearance, at most all they can do is continue to harass me with questions, all of which should be directed at him. He reminded me that teenagers run away all the time. The conversation makes me think of Jenny and ruins the entire day.

Even though I may have an idea about who might be at fault, what I don't have is proof or a motive, so I leave that part out of the discussion. What reason would Liam have to kidnap a kid, just because he made an off-colored comment? Particularly one that wasn't even directed at him.

If I really wanted to set the world spinning, I could mention Bobby Simmons, the guy who was run down in Austin, and the fact that Liam may have had good reason to kill both Monroe and his lover's fiancé. But what good would it do me?

I have a novel to finish, and seeing that Liam is doing more than half the work, I need him. And, also, I really don't have concrete evidence.

What I do have is time. If I finish the book and then tell the authorities what I know about Liam, no doubt a lot of press will come from it. I could certainly use the publicity. Even better if I can find a way to spin it into my novel. It is a mystery, after all. Why would a seemingly normal young man from a well-to-do family, with a burgeoning career, and his whole life ahead of him, murder two—three?—people? At best, this situation appearing at my doorstep turns out to be a red herring. At worst, a case study into the mind of a monster. There's only one question. Am I talented enough to write it in without Liam knowing I'm on to him?

I GREW UP SURROUNDED BY DEATH. MY FATHER WAS A HOMICIDE detective. His father was a mortician. I've long thought of the ways in which our fathers' careers have impacted the work we do in the world. My father's father ran a funeral home. My father grew up seeing grief on a daily basis, and I believe that is why he went into detective work. As for me, I grew up with a man married to his job, which was not abnormal for the times. He was gone a lot, and even when he was home, he often had that absent look in his eyes, like he was somewhere else entirely.

Sometimes I'd catch him looking at my mother or my sisters with such sadness written across his face that I had to look away. I imagined that he saw the faces of victims in them, and I imagine that fueled him more. I don't know that he looked at me that way; I hardly recall him looking at me at all. From an early age, he made it clear that I was to be the man of the house. I was in charge of caring for my mother and sisters while he was out doing important work in the world, or as he put it, keeping the wolves at bay.

Murder rarely occurs during business hours; it is usually between 10:00 p.m. and 3:00 a.m. So, on those days, his watch officially started when he arrived at the crime scene. He often didn't make it home until long after we were asleep. Sometimes I'd wake in the middle of the night and find him seated at the kitchen table, poring over court orders or reviewing search warrants.

Back then I don't think I appreciated how hard he worked; in fact, I know I didn't. It's difficult to understand what it's like to be a man with the weight of the world—and a family—on your shoulders until you are one and you have one. My father very rarely spoke of his work. He didn't share information about the cases he worked, and he didn't celebrate when he solved a case. He didn't buy into the cliché that he was a voice for the dead. He was a serious man with a serious work ethic. On occasion, I would see his files lying around and take a peek. Maybe it was the furtive nature of his job that made me fascinated with the dead and with writing about them. Maybe I just wanted to be closer to the man who lived down the hall but was, in many respects, a stranger. Maybe it's why I started making things up—to fill in the parts I never knew.

Any armchair psychologist worth their salt would suggest that I write mysteries because of my father's profession. If they dug a little deeper, they'd see that I don't just write mystery. I write easy mystery.

With my first novel, I was surprised. Truthfully, I didn't think it was all that good. I surely didn't think it would sell. It was actually Eve who packaged it up and mailed it to several agents. It was Eve who bought me my first good typewriter. She believed in me long before anyone else did, maybe even before I believed in myself. Without her, I would have moved on to something else, a profession my father found more respectable. He was embarrassed at having a son who made things up for a living. In fact, he was horrified that I spent my hours seated behind a typewriter conjuring the kind of stories he spent his life trying to stop.

Later, as my backlist grew and I became acquainted with my

audience, it made sense why my work has been successful, even if it can at times be considered predictable. People like to feel smart. There's nothing quite as satisfying as being right, proving that righteousness can be bottled and sold.

CHAPTER TWENTY-SEVEN

My eyes flutter open hesitantly. In the in-between of sleep and consciousness, I hear shuffling, something or someone stirring around me. Was it a part of my dream? Daylight hasn't yet broken, but there's just enough light peeking through the curtains that as my eyes adjust, I can see it wasn't a dream. A figure is standing over me. Instantly, I feel the pull, and my hands reach for my neck, toward the electrical cord that is wrapped around it. Digging into my skin, I try to get my fingers underneath the cord, but it's too tight. I can't.

"You're going to send me back to that place, I know it," she says calmly.

I try to call out to her, to say her name, but it comes out as a grunt. I try again and again to say something, to say anything, but speaking is impossible. Flinging my body from side to side like a fish out of water, I try to get a foothold.

"You want to kill me, George."

Again, I try to speak, to say her name, but words don't come, only a horrible gurgling sound. "Plea—"

"I'm sorry about this. But I can't let you send me back there. You promised."

Writhing back and forth, back and forth, I finally get enough momentum to swing my feet around, hanging them off the side of the bed. But then dizziness hits and I realize I am seconds away from passing out. It's funny how it isn't until words are taken from you that you realize how many you have left to say. I ask myself how she got out of that room. *Had I forgotten to lock the door? Had she planned this?*

Finally, I manage to push myself to an upright position. From there, I use my body weight to fling myself forward, putting a little distance between the two of us, just enough to get some slack on the cord. Eve is small, but when she gets like this, she might as well be ten feet tall and bulletproof. "What the fuck?" I ask when I can finally choke out words.

"I hate you!" she screams. "You're going to kill me. I know you are."

In the darkness I see her let go of the cord. She picks something up, and that's the last thing I see.

THE FIRST THING I NOTICE IS THE DULL ACHE IN MY BACK. THE second is the hard surface I'm lying on. It takes me a second to register what's happened. I ask myself what I know: My wife attacked me. *Eve. Where is she? What has she done?* Everything hurts. But I am on the outside of the pain—a detached observer. There's no fear, no other emotion, just my body instinctively willing me to get up. Rolling onto my side takes herculean effort. Somehow I manage.

I could easily and effortlessly give in to the desire to allow myself to sink back to sleep, although the bright morning light that filters in through the curtains making a zig-zag pattern next to me on the floor seems to beckon me toward the day. The warmth of the light sharpens my recollections, for a moment dulling the painful stiffness in my body.

I can't seem to erase the scene from my mind. My wife standing over me with a baseball bat, bringing it down, again and again.

I'm lying in the half-light, mentally wringing my hands, imagining all the things I could have done differently to avoid my present predicament, when the aroma hits me strong. It's not just the scent of blood, which is particularly pungent, but of something more pleasing. Something that makes my stomach clench and release several times over. Bacon.

It takes far longer than I think it will, but eventually I am able to army crawl my way over to the bed and pull myself to a kneeling position. From there I am able to hoist myself halfway onto the bed. My eyes are nearly fused shut, whether merely swollen or caked with blood, or both, I can't yet tell.

Blood is matted in my hair. There's a thick layer, dry and hardened, like hairspray, glued to my scalp. A six inch gash runs along the top of my skull. To the tips of my fingers, it feels wide enough to require staples.

With monumental effort, I make my way up to a standing position. My foot seizes up, nearly causing my knees to buckle. It's still sore from the knife wound, back when I thought our last incident was as bad as it could get. Although it's healing, it's tender. But at least I can hobble around halfway decently. Assessing my injuries with minimal visibility, I can feel that my left wrist is swollen about twice its normal size and—*fuck, is that a bone poking out?*

Instinct tells me to find Eve; logic tells me to fix my vision first. It takes an age to limp from the bed to the en suite bathroom, and another age still to wet a washcloth and carefully wipe the dried blood from my eyes. I peel it out of my eyelashes like dried paint.

The reflection staring back at me in the mirror is unrecognizable. My face is swollen, my nose clearly broken, and there's a bright red ring around my neck where the cord dug into my flesh. Although I suppose it could be worse. I could be dead.

Downstairs there's music playing, and over it, I hear a fair amount of rustling around in the kitchen. I'm terrified of what I will find, but whatever it is, at least I have confirmation that Eve is alive. The rest I will deal with once I get her locked in her room.

THE SPREAD IS REALLY SOMETHING, I'LL GIVE HER THAT. "GEORGE!" she says, glancing up, a distant look in her eyes. "Good, you're up."

She motions around the kitchen as a slow smile spreads across her face. "I've made breakfast. You must be starving."

I wish there were a manual, something to tell me how I'm supposed to handle this situation. Being with her, like this, is akin to a confrontation with a wild animal. "Eve," I say softly. "We have to talk."

Her whole body tenses. She reaches for a knife. My eyes flit toward the cottage. It's possible that this is going to go further south and that I am going to need Liam. Perhaps it's time for him to see what my wife is really like. Sure, I could call the police, but the odds of that turning out well are not in Eve's favor. In her current state, she's unpredictable, and the last thing I need is her getting shot.

What I need is to get her medicated. Then I can assess how to go about getting her the help she needs. "Let's sit." I point to the table. "You're right, I am hungry."

She looks at me like I'm a stranger standing in her kitchen. "What happened to your face?"

"You tell me."

Her lips part and she starts to speak before she stops herself. "How should I know?"

Pulling out a chair, I slowly ease myself down into it. Eve

places a plate in front of me. I consider how I'm going to get a sedative in her.

She takes the seat across from me and folds her hands, laying them on the table. Then she cocks her head. "You're bleeding, George."

I touch the tips of my fingers to my temple and pull them away, swiping the blood onto my napkin. "Yes."

She shakes her head and then stares down at her plate. "What a mess."

Picking through my eggs with my fork, I shuffle food around my plate. I'm not hungry. My head spins, making things come in and out of focus. The smell alone causes my stomach to turn. It threatens to empty at any second. The nausea hits in waves, but the pain is consistent. I need to think. I need to buy myself some time. I need to talk her into submission. In this condition, I won't be able to subdue her if she flies off the handle.

Eve jars me when she reaches out and slaps my good hand. "What are you doing?" she hisses. "We have to say our prayers first."

I drop the fork. In as many years as I've known my wife, I don't think I've ever seen her say grace. Although, I suppose this is as good a time as any.

CHAPTER TWENTY-EIGHT

How close to fire can you get without getting burned? That has become the question of my life. Liam's girl is back to stay, or so it appears, and Eve has been properly sedated. After breakfast she said she was exhausted and wanted to take a nap. I suppose this is to be expected when you've stayed up all night trying to kill your husband.

Once she was out cold, I shook her awake. Not fully awake, just so that she was coherent enough to lift her head while I held a glass of water to her lips. I placed a Haloperidol tab on her tongue and told her to swallow, aware that she'd be too eager to return to sleep to fight me on it.

Afterward, I went back to the kitchen and taped up my wrist. It's probably not broken—hopefully it's just a bad sprain—but in any case, the good news is, bones heal. I took several painkillers and then rinsed the dishes. I tidied up a bit, and then I watched the footage from last night, needing to determine how Eve had gotten out. Had I really forgotten to lock the door? Or had she suddenly become Houdini?

On the screen, I see myself come into focus. It's not the best system; I purchased it years ago. It's a baby monitor with a camera, black and white, paltry compared to what you can find on the market today. Nevertheless, I can't help but notice how old I look, how my age shows in my movement and in my body language. Hadn't I just run a marathon last year? Or was that two years ago now?

Time is a blur. A year ago, or last night, the only thing that's clear is the fact that my memory is failing me. On camera it becomes evident that I hadn't locked the door after I'd kissed Eve goodnight. Had I been drunk, tired, or just plain hopeful?

Anything's possible.

Whatever the case, I was distracted. It's excruciating, and as of late, irritating, to have a wife that's out of service. Being a long-term caretaker is not exactly what I had planned for my life.

I love Eve, obviously, and I understand what it means to make a vow to someone. But to live out that vow year after year, day after day, is proving to be another story entirely.

On an average day, by the time it comes to an end, even with Joni's help, there's not a lot left in me to put toward anything else. With work, and with managing the estate, and her care, not to mention all the little nuances of life, it's evident something has to give. Eve used to say this about mothering when the children were little, and sometimes I feel like maybe this is a form of payback. Only my wife is not a child. She's sick, and deteriorating rapidly.

You expect this sort of thing to occur naturally in life, growing old with a spouse. What no one tells you is how fast it actually happens. Even so, I'm not yet sixty, and on days where Eve's illness really gets to me, where her absence feels huge, or her presence unbearable, I can't help but think about what I'm missing out on. A normal life, whatever the hell that is.

Outside, across the yard, movement near the cottage catches my eye. Liam and the girl are cuddled up on the porch swing. It reminds me of Eve and I in years past. It reminds me of the reason I hung that swing in the first place. The countless evenings we spent in it and the few times we managed to take in a sunrise.

Liam sits upright, while she lies across his lap, her head resting in the crook of his arm. Another problem for me to fix. I glance at the clock. It reminds me, injured or not, I have to get some work in. A shower would do me good; I'll clean myself up as best I can. With any luck, I'll be able to locate some form of adhesive or glue around here to take the place of staples.

But my mind isn't focused on that. Not the way it should be. The girl reaches up and caresses Liam's face. On one hand, I'm glad she's back. Liam is more focused with her around. But her presence, while it has a positive effect on the writing front, also leaves me with one gigantic problem: how do I keep what happened between us under wraps, at least for the next couple of weeks? Until I can finish this manuscript and free myself of Liam. I weigh my options wondering what it's going to cost me to keep this mistake from him and from my wife just long enough for me to make it go away.

The most obvious answer would be to go straight to the source. Which is what I'd originally planned to do. But like I said, time has a way of marching on. As the saying goes, life is what happens when you're busy making other plans. There's also the fact that we've only seen each other from afar since Liam introduced us at the party. It's not that I haven't meant to find out what she wants and what she's up to; why she hasn't said anything, whether to me or to Liam, or to my wife, is a mystery in and of itself. It's not typical behavior, and generally where there's smoke there's fire. Is she afraid of Liam? And if so, what does she know?

GETTING TO THE HEART OF THE MATTER TURNS OUT TO BE EASIER than I thought. I emerge from the shower to a cacophony of noise. I rush to the window, thinking that Eve has escaped—that the police have surrounded the house, that if my life wasn't fucked before, it's certainly fucked now.

Only when I peel back the shutters, I'm only slightly relieved that's not what I see at all. There's a flurry of activity...the kind that can only mean one thing.

Liam has decided to throw another one of his parties.

To cheer her up, naturally.

I learn this the way I learn most things: after the fact. Out my window, there are teams of people working in unison, scattered amongst the property, rushing around hurriedly, making preparations. And it's white. As far as the eye can see. White flowers. White tents. White cushioned furniture. White gloves. You'd think he was having a goddamned wedding.

For a moment, I think maybe Eve really has killed me, and I'm about to witness my funeral.

Once I've dressed and tended to my injuries, I spend a good portion of the day sitting at my desk, attempting to write. This is how I know I'm not dead. It's strenuous, trying to work out the ending to this book. I thought I knew how things would turn out, but apparently my characters have different ideas in mind. With my head feeling the way it does and my eyes nearly swollen shut, I have a hell of a time staying focused on much of anything. My wrist throbs, and the rest of my body is stiff, but my mouth works just fine and I am at least able to dictate words into a recorder.

In the afternoon, with the turn of the key in the lock, I check in on Eve. She's drowsy on account of the sedative but awake as much as one could expect, considering. When I say I have something to tell her, she stares at me eagerly. I know I probably shouldn't do it. I should keep it to myself like the other stuff I don't want her to know. But I need her to know what's at stake if something were to happen, if she were to get out of this room, if she were to have an episode like the one she had last night. "I need you to remain calm," I tell her, patting her hand.

She peers up at me through sleepy eyes. Eventually her

scornful mouth curls upward. "I'm calm," she says, motioning around the small room.

She likes it in here. For me, it offers a creepy vibe, the kind that makes the hairs on the back of your neck stand on end. I've always gotten the feeling that something very bad once happened in here. At any rate, it was meant for storage, not to house a human. But we needed something without a window, something without objects that could be used for harm. "How could I possibly get more calm than this?"

"You're not going to believe it," I say. "It's about Liam."

Eve leans forward and rocks slowly back and forth. It's the meds. She seems to space out, to withdraw into herself, away from me, toward something else entirely, traveling somewhere I cannot reach. Eventually, she whips her head around and faces me. "She's back, isn't she?"

"Yes."

"Well, then," she says softly, almost too softly to hear, as though she's speaking only to herself. "I suppose we have to let them be."

"You're not feeling well," I tell her, rage suddenly boiling inside. "I'm going to put a stop to this. The last thing we need right now is a party."

"Just wait a second, George."

"What do you mean wait a second—what makes him think he can make decisions like this about our home? Without even consulting anyone?" I received an email from Liam which was supposed to serve as a consultation—maybe. He's put me back on the bestseller list. Now, he's planned a pre-release party for the new book. He says to "build excitement." What he really means is to bribe his friends and people in literary circles, to not only buy the book but to actually read it and speak positively about it. It's a big feat, I realize, but this seems like a bit much.

"I don't understand the point of parties," Eve tells me, her voice sounding very far off.

"Aside from the booze? Yeah, me either."

She shakes her head like she's trying to rattle a thought loose. "It's all for show."

Even when she's sick, my wife has a brilliant way of stating the obvious. In fact, I think it's her illness that makes her better at this than the rest of us. There's no pretense—just blatant honesty, a rare thing in this business and in life, and despite all the rest is one reason I can't seem to fall out of love with her. "That's why I just said—I'm going to put a stop to it."

"On the other hand," she says, turning toward me, her eyes brightening. "It could be fun."

"You hate parties."

"I think I can manage one more." I watch as she chews at her bottom lip until it bleeds. "He won't be here that much longer anyhow."

"This is a terrible idea."

"The best ones," she says, "usually are."

CHAPTER TWENTY-NINE

Eve insists I come down for a visit. She wants to see me before the party. Not that I plan to go anywhere near it, not in my condition. Instead, I plan to spend the night in my study, writing, inching ever closer to the finish line and to getting Liam off my property and out of my life. He apparently did more today than plan parties and canoodle. He worked, emailing me some outstanding notes, and also some feedback that I hadn't considered.

"I don't know why you keep saying that," Eve snaps. For most of the day, the sedative offered her the sweet release of sleep. But she's fully awake now, the waning meds and lowering sun having its usual effect on her. I promised to read her a little of the book before guests began arriving and I have to dose her again.

"Saying what?"

She lies back on the bed and draws her knees up, covering her eyes with her forearm. Her shorts hang off her hips, the bones jutting outward, visible beneath the sheets. She's lost weight. I know; I've spent many hours of my life studying the curve of those bones. "You keep referring to her as 'that girl.'"

I take her wrist from her eyes and place it at her side.

She glares at me, her brow furrowed. "I've seen her up close. She's hardly a girl."

I know better than to offer a response. No matter what I say, it will lead to trouble.

Eve props herself up on her elbows. "She's pretty, don't you think?"

"I hadn't noticed."

"Sure you have, darling," she says with a closed smile. "I saw your face when you were with her."

"I don't know what that means," I reply, drawing smooth circles with my finger on her knee. "For one, she's not my type. And two, even if she were, what does it matter?"

"A woman like that, dear, is everyone's type."

I lean toward her. "Interesting," I murmur against her neck. "But there's only one woman for me."

She pulls away. "Is that so?"

"How long have we been married?"

Her brows stretch toward the ceiling and her eyes follow suit. "A very long time."

"Then why do you insist on asking such silly questions?"

Eve scoots as far away from me as she can manage, forcing herself into a ball. "I'm tired, George."

"So rest."

"I'm not talking about that kind of tired. You know what I mean."

I stare down at the floor, singling out carpet fibers with my eyes, one by one. I've seen Eve pick them apart during a manic phase. It's not pretty. "We should replace this," I tell her with a nod.

"George?"

Our eyes meet. "Have you even heard anything I've said?"

"You're tired."

"Yes." Tears well up in her eyes. Finally, she sighs. "I don't want to do this anymore."

CHAPTER THIRTY

The party goes about the way I imagine. All I can think about is Eve locked in that room. About what she's done to me and about what I'm doing to her. About where this all ends. It's for the best, I realize, her being in there, safe. It sucks, nonetheless, to have people crawling all over my property, enjoying themselves, and my wife not be one of them.

She said this would be fun, otherwise I'd have put a stop to it, and even though I'd rather be doing just about anything else, she wasn't entirely wrong. After managing nearly a thousand words and partially editing several chapters, I step out onto the balcony that's off the great room. I bring along a drink and a cigar, even though I have no intention of lighting it. It's been ages since I smoked, but there's something about rolling one between my fingers that I can't let go of.

Kicked back under the stars, I am surprised to find myself enjoying the party from afar. Eavesdropping can be very enlightening. I'm three drinks deep and overlooking the lawn when I hear a familiar voice behind me. "It's strange, isn't it?"

I don't have to turn in my chair to know who it is. But that doesn't stop me. Her long hair swept up, my wife is right—she is pretty. She's wearing a dress, black, not as short as the last time. "Whatever you're speaking of," I say, "I'm sure the answer is yes."

"It's funny," she sighs whimsically. "We can be so together and yet so alone."

I watch her hands as she pulls a cigarette from her clutch, sticks it between her lips and then fishes for a lighter. "You mind?"

I shrug.

She takes a long pull and exhales into the night air. "For millennia, people have taken vacations...people have had children..." she tells me, like she's getting at some great big point. "This is an endless universe which spans who knows how long." She gestures toward the sky, and I consider for a moment that she's had too much to drink. "And still people think the details of their lives are special. So much so that they go to parties and spend the whole night detailing them to complete strangers." She takes another drag, this time blowing smoke my way. It reminds me how much I miss it, regardless of the source. "No one is that special, George."

Nostalgia rolls off her tongue in a manner I find amusing. "I take it you're not a fan of people."

"Oh, I love people," she quips. "It's the niceties and fakery I could do without."

I don't say anything in response, even though I understand what she means completely. I had been thinking it myself. As a collector of stories, I sometimes get so wrapped up in my own little world that I forget what it's like. Back when I was a regular chart-topper, there were endless social functions, awards, book tours and such. It always struck me as odd that strangers felt that because they knew my words, they knew me. To describe what it was like standing there talking to people who felt like they knew me but who were essentially strangers, as far as I was concerned, is awkward. They'd ask me about the children, about life, picking out small details in articles, piecing them together, painting sometimes, but not often, accurate pictures of my life.

I never felt more like an imposter than I did standing there listening to people drone on incessantly about their trip to Italy three summers ago or little Johnny's latest feat.

"It makes me feel like a fraud. All this smiling."

"I heard about your fiancé."

She turns to face me. "Absolutely tragic, isn't it?"

"The death of a young person is always tragic."

"Oh, I don't know if I'd go that far."

I swirl the remaining whiskey around my glass. "The cops have any leads?"

"For all I know," she says with a snicker, "they're watching me this very second."

"Who could blame them?"

"We weren't married." She leans against the balcony. "What motive could I possibly have?" she asks, giving me the side-eye. "It's not like I've gained anything."

"Freedom isn't nothing."

"True," she smirks. "Good thing I have an airtight alibi."

"That's smart."

I watch as she stubs her cigarette out. "Aren't you going to ask me what I was doing?"

"No."

"Why not?"

"It's none of my business. And to be honest, I really don't care."

"Oh George," she laughs. It's a head back, throaty kind of laugh. Then she looks me in the eye. "That's where you're wrong. You should care. You should care very much."

"Should I?"

A smile lights up her whole face. The kind of smile that makes me unsure whether I want to kill her or fuck her. "I told them I was with you."

CHAPTER THIRTY-ONE

At this point in my life, there's not much that she could say that would surprise me. But if a reaction is what she was after, a reaction was what she got. Mid-sip, I nearly spit out my whiskey. Afterward, she sits down beside me and lowers her voice. It's full of smoke and mischief. "I think we could be very good together, you and I."

"I'm married. And my wife is asleep downstairs."

"That didn't stop you before."

I down my drink. She isn't wrong.

"You know your characters in *When Tomorrow Ends*, Jen and Harry?"

"Sure."

"I want a love like theirs."

I wouldn't be so sure about that, I think but don't say. "It's fiction."

"Maybe," she shrugs. "But I don't buy it."

"Apparently, you already did."

"You got me," she answers with a frown. "What happened to your face?"

"I don't want to talk about it." I stand with the intention of refilling my glass. "Why are you here anyway? You shouldn't be here."

She shakes her head slowly from side to side. "You're right. I don't want to talk about any of that stuff either." My eyes move toward her legs as she crosses and uncrosses them. Is she being suggestive? Or trying to get comfortable? She smiles that smile again, letting me know it's the former. "I want to talk about us."

"There is no us."

She glares up at me and cocks her head. "Who are you trying to convince?"

HOW I END UP IN THE GUEST BATHROOM WITH THE GIRL PROPPED UP on the sink is anybody's guess. Although I suppose when you mix alcohol and loneliness, it isn't so hard to imagine. "You know, George," she tells me afterward, "I've always been your number one fan."

I wash up, while simultaneously strategizing my exit. "I don't think you should tell Liam."

"Liam who?"

"Seriously."

She fixes her dress and then checks her face in the mirror. "Okay. Whatever."

"I think he can be dangerous."

She cocks her head. "What?"

"Just don't say anything," I tell her fumbling with my belt. "And stay away from my wife."

Putting herself between me and the sink, placing her hands on either side of my broken up face, she looks me in the eye. "I want to have your baby."

I don't know if I'm surprised. But I realize in that moment just how much more I have bitten off than I can chew. *Fuck. Fuck. Fuck.* This one isn't just trouble; she's smart.

I'm actually kind of impressed. She's offering me the only thing that I really want. A career comeback is all I've been focused on for months—years, if I really think about it. But why? It's not for the accolades.

It's for the legacy.

I've spent my entire career chasing that, because I know, after I'm dead and gone, nothing besides my work will be left behind. Every part of me that was supposed to exist in the future, the parts that were supposed to carry on long after I'm gone, are dead.

"Imagine it, George," she murmurs. "A little boy—or a girl—who cares? Imagine them running around this place."

The problem is I can imagine it. It's the best and the worst idea I've ever heard. I shake my head, but the questions keep coming. How do you weigh the two? That which you know is wrong but also feels very right? How do you make the choice between your head and your heart? Is it even possible trying to please someone outside of you while trying to please what's on the inside at the same time? "Please tell me you're on contraception."

"Only time will tell."

I push her against the sink. It hurts my back. It hurts everything. "This isn't funny."

"Isn't it?"

I need a drink. "No."

"You know what I think, George?"

"I'm sure you're going to tell me regardless."

She smiles. "I think this is humor on a cosmic level."

CHAPTER THIRTY-TWO

I haven't set foot in the cottage in a long time. I wouldn't be doing so now except for the fact that I can't sleep, and I need to talk to Liam. I have to put a stop to him and his parties, even if they are self-serving, even if he is bribing his rich friends to buy my book and to talk about it to their rich friends.

This, and he needs to keep the girl away. I have to let him know this without saying why. He's not allowed to invite her back here. She needs to stay away from me and away from my property.

The easiest way to fix the problem is to let him know that it's time he moved himself back to the city. He's worn out his welcome. As it is, I am having a hard enough time keeping the situation with Eve under wraps, and I don't need it leaking out and somehow finding its way to my publisher, or worse, to the press. Not that they care all that much about me, but still. They're more than welcome to write whatever they want about me and my drinking, about me behaving badly online, but my wife is off limits.

By the time I reach the steps, I am fuming. It's four in the morning and the place is lit up like a Christmas tree. I know the girl isn't here—at least she's not supposed to be. She said she was driving back to the city on account of business. What kind of business, she did not offer up, but I'm pretty sure Liam mentioned once that she works in public relations. It seems altogether fitting, even though she doesn't strike me as someone who intends to be a part of the working class for long.

Two raps and I twist the doorknob. Maybe I've had a few drinks, plus a painkiller or two, but then, maybe I'm just angry. My give-a-fuck meter is running on empty. This is my goddamned house; I'm not going to wait outside like I'm the guest.

Turning the handle, I'm both annoyed and surprised to find the door locked. I knock once again, but the music is loud and it's doubtful Liam can even hear me over all of this nonsense.

When I go to bang on the thick cedar door a fourth time, I remember the spare key under the potted plant on the side of the cottage. It takes a bit of fumbling around in the dark, but eventually I locate it and open the front door.

I don't know what I was expecting to find. Or honestly, what I expected the outcome to be. I just know it wasn't this.

"GEORGE!" LIAM EXCLAIMS OVER THE BUMPING MUSIC. HIS VOICE IS at full bore, straining the muscles in his chiseled neck. "Would you mind turning that down and giving me a hand?"

I back away, stepping over the threshold, nearly tripping out the door. "Good God," he says, removing one of his gloves. "What the fuck happened to you?"

"Car accident."

"Today? Right now? Is that why you missed the party?"

I shake my head and continue in the opposite direction. "Doesn't matter."

"George," he says, his voice tinged with concern. "Are you all right? You seem—"

"Where is she?" I ask as my eyes survey the mess: the blood and the plastic sheeting and the dripping saw.

He smears his gloved hand against his apron. "Who? Leslie?" Blood coats the front of it. A lot of blood. "She went back to the city."

"Who's that?"

"Ah," he says, turning back to the body parts laid out on the plastic. "That's no one."

I'm going to be sick. Right there at his feet, imminently, he's about to have more cleaning up to do. "What have you done?"

"I think you may have hit your head. Come here," he motions. "Let's take a look. Are you bleeding?"

I scan the living room. There's an arm and a leg, and part of something...it's all strewn about like pieces to a puzzle. Upon closer inspection, I try to see if I can find any indication that it might be Leslie. There are tufts of blonde hair and the limbs are fair skinned and slim, although other than that I can't make out anything discernible. But then, I can't locate a head.

"Do you know how much blood a person can lose before they die, George?"

He's talking about exsanguination. I first learned about it after Eve was attacked in college. I'd wanted to know how close I'd actually come to losing her. Pretty close, as it turns out.

"Two and a half to four liters on average," I say. "But it depends on several factors."

His bottom lip juts out. "Such as?"

"Whether we're talking about a child or an adult, for one. And the size of the person."

"I like you, George," he tells me, and I know if a person says your name this many times they're trying to sell you on something, and probably in this case, worse. "I've always liked you."

"Look," I hold my hands up, palms facing him. "I'm going to get back to the house. I was just coming over to ask you to turn the music down. That and, well, the accident. I'm feeling a bit confused. Maybe a concussion..."

"I think we need to get you checked out."

"In the morning," I say. "I assume you'll get this taken care of and cleaned up?"

"Assumptions are always a bad idea."

"My father was a homicide detective," I tell him. "Did you know that?"

"I know everything about you, George."

Not everything. "Well, then you must know that over the past ten years, there have been three hundred and forty-seven murders."

"That's a lot."

"Yeah—and there are approximately two hundred and fifty-one open cases which are still not solved."

He shrugs. "What's your point?"

"Homicide detectives tend to be some of the most committed officers in any agency. But they can't solve a case without the community's help, and the truth is, as you know, not every case gets solved."

"What does this have to do with me?"

"It's math, Liam. Simple math. Each year detectives solve anywhere between 60-70% of homicide cases, but only about 30-40% are from that calendar year."

"Okay." He walks toward me. "But just because it isn't solved doesn't mean the case isn't being worked."

"That's my point. They may not catch you now, but eventually, they will."

CHAPTER THIRTY-THREE

'The Book Doctor'

Journal Entry

She was drunk. And worse, she wasn't invited. I could describe her, but it's probably easiest just to say she was the kind of woman who was insufferable and leave it at that.

She was mostly sober by the time she finally died. At least I think. It was a thousand little cuts at first. She thought I wanted sex, but no. I wouldn't have. Couldn't have. For one, I'd already been intimate with Leslie, and even then, I don't want to cheat, not anymore. And if I were to do so, it wouldn't be with someone like that.

It took a lot to tie her up, but not that much. What I mean by that is at first she let me. Fetishes for the win! But then I realized, seeing as I couldn't have her running off into the night half-dead, that a few zip ties probably weren't going to cut it. Pun intended.

Anyway, after I wore myself out getting her securely tied, I had to spread out all of the plastic sheeting. Better not to do it beforehand. Fetish or not, most people tend to shy away from that sort of thing. It can be a bit much. Unless you're a neat freak, which I am. OCD leaves little room for real fun. Still, I try.

Once I got the plastic all laid out, I realized I hadn't sharpened my tools. A rookie mistake, but when you're busy, you're busy. Plus, I'd had another method in mind for killing her and only changed my mind at the last second. It was a great party, but it left me feeling empty and bored. I needed a little excitement, and simple asphyxiation just wasn't going to cut it. Gah, the puns. I can't help myself. I'm delirious. It's late, or rather early, and I should be sleeping. This, and Leslie is back in my life. We made love, and it was everything I wanted it to be.

Since I couldn't sleep, I needed something time consuming, something to fill the hours until Leslie came back to me, and the insufferable, uninvited party girl turned out to be it.

How many organs can you trench out before a person dies? How much skin can you peel away? How much flesh can you remove from bone? As long as you don't nick a main artery, it's more than you'd think. Four hours' worth of amusement, this one got me.

Although that doesn't mean it was all fun and games. With all of her crying and begging, she was intolerable until the very end. I should have made it come sooner.

CHAPTER THIRTY-FOUR

I have no idea how our story ends, but this cannot be it. Hard as I tried, I couldn't manage to get out of that cottage and back to the illusion of safety in my own home. Not without Liam in tow. Of course I couldn't. That would have been too easy. More and more, I am learning, nowhere is safe and nothing is easy.

He's going to kill me. That much isn't too hard to work out. After I found him in the cottage, hacking up all the limbs, he marched me straight back here to my office. Now he wants me to write out the scene in detail. Also, then he's going to finish me off.

In this kind of situation, what you need to do is assess how important you are to another person getting what they want. That will tell you your odds of survival.

The more you are needed, the more likely you are to survive. I've witnessed firsthand how talented Liam is. He hardly needs me. He's already wealthy, and he can write. He has the chops. I'm just a cog in the wheel of whatever game it is he's playing. A chess piece. A blip on his radar as he makes his way to the top. That's the thing about rich people, especially those who also have talent. They're endlessly restless. Always looking for something, or someone, to sink their teeth into. And why wouldn't they? Their basic needs are easily met; how else are they supposed to fill all those hours?

Imagine the press the book will get when I end up dead. Is that what he's after? What else could it be, if not the fame and attention?

Fame is dangerous, that way. It'll get you every time. The thrill of acclaim, of having people think you've done something worthwhile. It's a double-edged sword, notoriety, as evidenced by my current predicament. Liam doesn't know this yet, but he will someday. There will always be someone smarter, someone younger, someone with more talent.

All you can do is ride the wave when it comes and keep your head down after it passes. If only I'd been better at the latter.

"You know," he says, slapping the back of my head, the force of which causes blood to spray from my lips. "It really can't get much worse."

Surveying the blood that coats my desk, I beg to differ.

He spins the chair around until I good and truly can't see anything. Then, he smacks me with the barrel of the gun. The crack reverberates from ear to ear, bouncing around inside my skull like a snare drum. "Write."

When I can manage and not a moment sooner, I flex my fingers. Stretch and flex. Flex and stretch. It's a scene he is used to, which is maybe why he elbows me in the face. My mouth fills with blood. I spit a broken tooth onto the keyboard. "I told you. I can't."

"You are going to die," he tells me. "Either way, you are. *How* it happens is up to you."

When he moves to strike again, I lean away. This time, I hold my hands up in surrender. I relent. "Okay…just give me a minute."

I watch in relief as he shoves the gun in the waist of his tuxedo pants. He walks toward the door, and I think this is where it ends, but I ought to know him better than that. With a smile, he lifts a plastic bag from the floor and raises it until it's eye level. "Do you know what this is?"

I'm a writer. I'm afraid I might.

He pulls out a container of lighter fluid and then another and another, counting as he tosses the empty bottles onto the floor. When the bag is empty, he drops it and fetches a book of matches from his coat pocket. On the front, the name of the restaurant where we had our first meeting. "Don't worry," he says. "It'll go quick."

My eyes dart toward the door. "Listen—"

As he watches me contemplate my next move, a grin spreads across his face. He knows I'm thinking about what's at stake if I don't make it out of this room alive.

She will die. She will burn to death, and while he will have been the one to set the house ablaze, we both know this is a fire that started long before he struck the match.

"You see. This is what happens when a person doesn't know their own limits."

He's wrong. It's the dead of night, and even if I could manage the mile and a half it takes to reach the neighbors, it would be too late.

"You can't save everyone," he says, confirming my suspicion. "That's the problem nowadays. Everybody wants to be the hero."

He lifts me by the throat and drags me across the office. I could ask why he doesn't just put a bullet in my head and be done with it, but I don't have to. That would ruin the ending.

"It could have gone differently, you know."

I hold my breath as I crane my neck. There's a car coming up the drive. Is it her? Is she coming back? Has she ruined my life, only to save it?

Soon enough, I realize I am mistaken. No one is coming to save me. It's only wishful thinking. Hope will suffocate you if you let it.

My eyes flit toward the gun. His attention is on the door. That's always been his weakness, his distractibility.

He tears off a match and drags it along the rough edge of the matchbook. "I know what you're thinking..."

What I'm thinking is I've spent some time in burn units doing research. Even if I didn't love Eve, even if I could hate her for what she's done, inviting him into our home, I don't want her to die this way.

The match ignites. At the halfway point, he leans forward and stubs it out on my hand. I move to block him, to go for the gun, and as I do my hand grazes my face in the process. Bile rises in my throat. What was once my jawline is now just flesh hanging.

"It's okay," he says, shoving me toward the sofa. "None of it will matter when you're dead."

"You don't—"

"Now is not the time for bargaining..." He strikes another match. "Really, you should be thanking me. At least she won't have to see you like this."

My brow furrows, giving me away. I don't mean for it to happen. My poker face has a habit of betraying me where she is concerned. Automatic response is inevitable, and if distraction is his weakness, she is mine.

I'm half-seated, half-slumped on the couch when he pulls the gun from his waistband and aims it at my head. "I thought you'd be more comfortable here." He motions toward the notepad beside me. "Now write."

"You might as well just shoot me."

Before the sound of the gun firing registers, I feel the white-hot searing pain. Before I feel the white-hot searing pain, I see bone fragments fly from my kneecap. The blood makes me realize I should have made an effort.

Later, when I come to, I hear a mewling sound somewhere deep in the belly of the house. Maybe it's her. Maybe it's me. Maybe I'm dead, and maybe this is hell.

He's seated cross-legged on the floor in front of me, gripping the gun in one hand, picking pieces of bone out of the carpet with the other. "The things you make me do."

I watch as he spreads the pieces of my knee out in front of him and begins fitting them together like a jigsaw puzzle. "Not bad, eh?" He flashes a smile. "What do you think?"

What I'm thinking is maybe it's impossible to survive a man like him.

"Now that you're awake," he says, "it's time to finish the story."

"I—"

"Don't. Remember? You promised."

He's right. I did promise.

That's how this started.

"*You* finish it," I say.

"That would negate the purpose of all of this—of me shooting you in the knee—of me wasting my precious time trying to help your ass out of a very big jam." He shakes his head. "And look at the thanks I get." That smile of his, the one that has undoubtedly always gotten him what he wants, he flashes it. "You really wouldn't want this to have all been for nothing, would you?"

I type a few words out just to see what comes to mind. *This is not how it ends.*

"You see, George. This is good." He squeezes my shoulder. "Now you're learning to finish what you start."

CHAPTER THIRTY-FIVE

Flames lick my skin. Metaphorical flames at first and then real ones. Meanwhile, I type and I type and I type. Liam tells me he wants to see what it's like to watch a person burn to death. Slowly, apparently.

"That's an okay start," he says, glancing over my shoulder at my screen. "Now, keep going."

Nothing will satisfy him, I realize. I can only keep going, trying to cross some invisible finish line. He lights match after match, putting it out on my skin. At the same time, he asks absurd questions. I answer them in hopes that it will buy me some time. In hopes that it will save Eve.

Another match lit, another flame put out. This time behind my ear. I have no leverage here, hardly a shot at seeing daylight. It strikes me as odd that all of my sunrises are now behind me. All that's left are my words and the answers he demands.

Liam is careful with the matches. One wrong move and the room goes up in flames. Empty lighter fluid bottles are littered across the floor. "How many ribs are in a human body?"

I type a sentence and delete. Nothing seems right when you know the words are going to be your last. "Twenty-four."

"How many joints?"

"In the body?"

He slaps the back of my head. "You can't answer a question with a question." Striking another match, he says, "Of course in the body." He puts it out, this time on my inner ear. The sound of my own skin sizzling makes my stomach turn. "Don't fuck with me. Answer the question."

"Two hundred and thirty."

Liam exhales loudly. "How much skin does a person shed in their lifetime?"

"Roughly forty pounds."

"Roughly forty pounds," he mocks in a sing-song voice.

I watch as he crosses the room. He sinks down on the couch. I wonder how long this can go on. How many questions can he have?

He rests his head back and stares up at the ceiling. "How many gallons of blood flow through your kidneys in a day?"

"About four hundred."

His face reddens and then he looks over at me. "How the fuck do you know all of this? You were a lit major."

"I read a lot."

"Fine," he says, repositioning himself on the sofa. "What was the name of the serial killer who dressed up as a clown and worked charity events?"

"John Wayne Gacy."

"Goddamn it." He slaps his leg. After taking a deep breath in, he slowly exhales. "The St. Valentine's Day Massacre is associated with which famous criminal?"

My patience is wearing thin. "What is this? Trivia night?"

Apparently his, too. He practically flies off the couch and rushes me, grabbing the gun from his waistband in the process. He presses it to my temple. "Is that your final answer?"

"Al Capone," I cough. Rolling my eyes, I add, "Allegedly. Technically, it remains an unsolved crime."

He thinks for a moment, chewing at his bottom lip. "Who was the most prolific known serial killer in United States history?"

I know the answer, of course. But I'm over his games. I draw it out a little, stammering as I reply, "Samuel Little or Harold Shipman. Authorities aren't sure of actual victim counts."

"This makes no sense." His face twists into a perplexed frown. "No one ever gets these."

"Not no one," I say, eyeing the door as I consider making a break for it. I'd lose, but almost anything would be better than this. Even a bullet. Even my skin melting off.

"Killer H.H. Holmes had a house in Chicago that eventually bore what nickname?"

"Murder Castle."

He closes his eyes, and by the time he opens them, he doesn't look like himself. He looks like another person. He morphs before my eyes in the way that I've seen Eve do during one of her manic phases. "Fuck!"

I watch as he paces the office. He takes the manuscript I printed and lights page after page on fire. I look on as my last words disappear before my eyes. Every few steps he stops and looks over at me, hopeful. "What's the name of the serial killer who claimed that a demonic dog commanded him to commit murder?"

"David Berkowitz."

This time his face isn't angry. He cocks his head. He's curious. "What kind of dog?"

"A Labrador Retriever."

The questions, they keep coming. I answer them all. With each question, he grows more and more frustrated. He can't kill me until I get one wrong. Something about it going against his principles, he says. I realize that I am going to burn to death before he puts a bullet in my head. So finally, I put the nail in the coffin. "I slept with your girlfriend."

CHAPTER THIRTY-SIX

It burns. It burns and it burns and it burns. Forcing my eyes open, it's evident the flames have grown since the last time. In and out of consciousness I mingle, going back and forth, grasping at life, welcoming death. I hear sirens, so many sirens. I think of Eve and I wonder if I'll see her in heaven.

I don't think I will.

If there is such a thing, I don't think that's where I'm going.

I feel lucky that we've had these years together. Lucky that we met in the first place. It's a great big world, and yet, somehow by mere chance, the two of us were thrust together. What are the odds of that, being in the same place at the same time on any given day, falling in love, and spending your life with a person?

Maybe it's the closer I get to death and the further I get from life, but suddenly it all feels like a dream. As though my mind has been sucked into a time machine. A vortex of thought, seemingly related and unrelated, I am like a clock winding down.

It's early, and I see her there in the library, her nose scrunched up, her finger entangled in a loose strand of hair. She twirls and unfurls the same piece of hair over and over for hours. After a while she looks up at me and smiles. She must have felt me watching her. I smile back and she offers a little wave. I go over to her and I say, "I have a story to tell you."

Her face is eager as she leans across the table and pulls out a chair. I sit down and she says, "Tell me everything. I want to hear it all."

So I tell her the story of us. As I speak, she inches closer, propping her elbow on the table, resting her head in the palm of her hand. I see the whole world in her eyes, and I know that's where the future is.

After I get through the beginning and the heavy middle, finally I come to the end. I tell her I'm sorry. I tell her that if she were to ask the people who knew us, they would say we lived a full life. We loved. We went through it. They'd say we weren't perfect, but man, we were something.

She looks at me all funny-like when I thank her. She laughs in that shy way she used to before the end, before the heavy middle, back before things got rough. She says, "You're crazy."

I tell her she's wrong.

"Why would I agree to dinner with you?" she asks. "Let alone fall in love?"

I tell her that since I can see the future, that she has no choice.

"What's in the future?"

She wants to know, so I tell her. I say, "You made me feel safe. Safe enough to be who I wanted to be."

I say, "Your love gave me such a platform to go and make an impact on the world."

I tell her our marriage gave me the energy to go out there and do the things I wanted to do.

I say, "I made a bigger impact on the world because of the energy your love gave me."

"So you want to be famous," she says. "That's what this is all about?"

"No," I tell her. "I just don't want to be obscure."

"What does that even mean?"

"I want my life to have meant something."

"Well," she says finally. "Did it?"

"Yes." I reach for her hand. I expect her to pull away, but she doesn't. "You made me feel like I wasn't alone in the world. And I don't just mean because we had each other. I mean because you saw me. You got me."

"Anybody could do that."

"No," I say. "They can't. There's a certain existential loneliness in life. Your ability to see me made me feel less alone in the world."

"This is getting sappy," she says.

"But we're going to die," I tell her. "So what does it matter?"

"I don't want to die."

"We don't have a choice. We invited him in, and this is what happens when you aren't careful."

Just then, Liam barges through the door. It doesn't make any sense, because he isn't supposed to be there in that library. He belongs in the future.

"Time means nothing," he says. He sticks the gun to my head and he pulls the trigger.

"George," Eve calls out. "Oh God, George." She clasps one hand over her mouth, her words muffled, filtered as they come out. "Oh God, what have you done?"

It's him, I try to say, but can't because most of my face is blown off. *He does bad things.* I need her to understand, but I don't think she ever does.

She opens her mouth to speak but all that comes out are screams.

CHAPTER THIRTY-SEVEN

I don't remember being pulled from the fire. The last thing I recall was Liam putting the gun to my chin and firing. And Eve's face. I remember that. I recall hearing the sirens. God, there were a lot of sirens.

Maybe there was Joni's voice. I hear she's the one who found us. My memory of the events of those early morning hours is questionable. My memory of most things is hazy.

There's a lot of white in this place. It's like a hospital, but different. Austin Lakes Hospital, they call it. All dressed up, it sounds fancy. Like a spa. Believe me, it isn't.

The doctor comes in to see me. There are a lot of doctors here, but not like the kind in a real hospital. They don't fix you. They only want to talk. This guy is new; I haven't seen him before. At least I don't think.

He sits across from me and studies me intently. He crosses and uncrosses his legs. He watches the door, like he's running down the clock. When he does speak to me, it's pointless. I can't speak back.

But then, I suppose a lot of his patients are that way.

What I can do is chicken peck at keys, when I'm allowed, but even that is iffy. I have burns over seventy percent of my body, my fingers and hands included.

"Shall we get started?"

I would laugh if I had the part of my face required to do so. Him with his formalities. Him with his fancy pen. I don't like the look of him. I don't like the look of any of them. It's a problem that can be remedied, unlike the rest of them. He probably won't come around again.

He introduces himself by name. I'm not sure if I'm imagining it, but he looks like Liam. Same hair. Same funny clothes. I don't want to see Liam in this place.

He's everywhere.

Suddenly, I hear Eve's voice. *So he's like a book doctor, then?*

I don't think it's supposed to make me sad, but it does.

The doctor goes through the usual spiel, saying the same thing they always say. Eventually, he hands me a tablet so that I can type my answers. It says a lot about him, that he bothers to go through the motions. As though he's changed his mind. He's hopeful.

He's determined that there will be answers.

He is wrong.

For a long time, they have tried. They keep asking me questions.

I have nothing to say.

Supposedly, Eve has told them enough.

"You have killed people, George," he remarks solemnly. "Can you tell me what that's like?"

My fingers twitch involuntarily. This question is one no one has asked. Maybe this is why I'm inclined to answer.

I type out, *Liam.* They always get this part wrong, and then I can't talk to them anymore.

"You killed Liam?"

I tap the question mark key. I don't know if I killed Liam. I don't think I did. But then, a lot of what I once thought was true is now up for grabs.

"You're a writer."

Was.

"Maybe you could write your story."

No.

"Maybe Liam could write it then?"

I don't know what Liam can do. He's capable of anything. I don't write this. He won't understand. They never do.

Instead, I only type one more word. But it's enough. *Eve.*

"You want me to tell you about Eve?" he asks.

Yes. I wasn't expecting him to say that. I know enough but they never tell me anything new.

"Eve is in another facility across town."

He means another hospital, but they never say this. Eve is in the state hospital. I hear it's worse than this one.

She's sick and she hates people, I type out. *This is the worst thing that could happen.*

"It's not the worst, though, is it?"

I don't know what he means.

"You murdered a lot of people over many years, George."

No matter how many times I tell them it was Liam, they never listen. Sometimes he visits me here, but they say I'm lying about that too.

"Has anyone ever explained dissociative identity disorder to you, Mr. Dawson?"

They have, of course. There's no point in wasting my energy typing that out, so I just stare at him. Even a nod would be too much to manage.

"Dissociative identity disorder, previously called multiple personality disorder, is usually a reaction to trauma, as a way to help a person avoid bad memories. It is generally characterized by the presence of two or more distinct personality identities. Each may have a unique name, personal history, and characteristics."

I know this. The treatment is talk therapy, which is why I'm sitting here.

"You held your wife against her will for years."

I don't know why he is saying any of this.

Maybe I am dreaming. Maybe I am dead.

Eve is sick, I summon the energy to type this out.

"I can't speak to Eve's health. I'm here to talk about yours."

He shifts in his chair. I hope the clock has run out. I have a good book that needs getting back to. "I'd like to study you, George. Maybe your story could help other people."

Where is Liam? Is he dead?

"You tell me."

I don't know.

"You're a very successful storyteller, Mr. Dawson. You also committed horrific crimes. I would like to learn about them."

It was Liam. He framed me.

"No, George. You are Liam."

They all say this. But Liam is young and...different. It doesn't make any sense. It probably doesn't even matter.

I want to see my wife.

"I have an idea. Why don't you write to her instead? I'll talk to her doctors, and if it makes sense, maybe you can exchange letters."

Even though he is lying, I write. I write and I write and I write. It takes a very long time, but once my fingers start, they don't stop. No matter how long it takes, I have to tell Eve the story. I need her to know that I'm sorry I couldn't read her the rest of it. I'm sorry I couldn't finish. I tell her why. Because I never wanted it to end.

MUCH TO MY AMAZEMENT, THE DOCTOR DOES COME BACK. He brings me books. Interesting books. Novels I've read, but many I haven't. He says he's come to help me finish my story. But then, that's what they all say.

He reads my words to Eve.

One day, he says. "Is that what you fear, George? Death? Losing everything? Is that why you created Liam?"

I did not create Liam. He just is.

"Nothing really ends though, does it?" the doctor says.

I don't know. When you rule things out you limit your focus.

"I've heard that somewhere before. Maybe in one of your books."

Probably.

"Eve says you were seeing another woman. That you saw lots of women. But that you always killed them. She admits to helping you plan up your crimes. She thought it was for your books. Until she realized they were coming true."

Eve is sick.

"Did this start after the death of your children? Trauma can have profound effects."

It started when I met Liam.

"It can also be brought on by extreme stress. Were you under a lot of stress? You had to have been."

I don't know.

"You were about to go bankrupt and lose your home. Not only were you having financial problems, but you were struggling to care for your wife. Your publisher was about to take you to court..."

Yes.

"We believe you created Liam to help you compensate."

Trying to make a crazy person understand they're crazy is a losing game. Believe me, I know.

You can't understand crazy, it just is. I don't type this. It would be disrespectful to his profession. And he holds the keys to a lot of things. My connection to Eve and my reading material being a couple of important ones. Instead I write, *we want to assign motives to things but we can't. What we would do in any given situation is not necessarily what someone else would do. Especially not a crazy person.*

"So what you're saying, George, is you're not meant to be understood."

Maybe nothing is.

"But that doesn't stop us from trying. It's normal and it's healthy to seek answers."

Answers change. Nothing is static.

"Why did you and your wife kill people? Did Liam tell you to?"

No, Liam acted on his own.

"So your wife didn't know?"

I don't think so.

"She says you planned the murders. You wrote about them and read her the stories. She said that you'd throw parties afterward to celebrate. She also says that a lot of your crimes are detailed in your work."

I tap the question mark key.

"Your father was a detective, right? That had to have made an impact on you. Being so close to crime at such a young age. I'm sure you learned a few things too—about how cases are—or aren't —solved."

I don't answer, so he goes on.

"You've written thirty-eight books. That's a lot of murders. Are there more victims?"

He's asking me things I can't possibly know. *You're going to have to ask Liam.*

"Where is he? And when can I meet him?

I don't know. He just shows up.

CHAPTER THIRTY-EIGHT

My days pass slowly. In some ways, life is no different than it was before. I wake up, I write. I read. I go to sleep. I do the same thing over again the next day. The only thing that's missing is my wife.

At night when I can't sleep, I lie awake and think of Eve. There's a light outside my room; it's bright and it flickers. No one knows exactly what it does, or what purpose it's supposed to serve. I've asked. It seems people don't like to answer my questions. That's Liam's fault too. Anyway, it reminds me of a call light on an airplane, only it's large, with a yellow-green hue. It reminds me of a light I installed in Eve's room, so that she wouldn't be scared in the dark.

When I first arrived, all I could think about was making it go away. Whatever it took, I just needed a way to find sleep. But the more I studied it, as the nights went on, the more I watched it pulsate, the more I realized everything has its rhythm. Everything has a story to tell. And everything eventually finds its way back around.

Often I lay awake, timing my words and my thoughts to the

cadence of that light. I wonder if Eve has something similar outside her door. I hope she does.

The only good thing about our separation is I have more time to write. My publisher signed me for a three-book deal. Funny how that works out. I can't receive the royalties, of course. They go to a fund for the victims' families. I have another book in mind, but before I sign a deal for that one, I'm throwing in a caveat. Some of the money has to go toward upgrading Eve's care. I have a feeling that'll work itself out. These things usually do.

Eve was big into yoga before the kids. Before life got out of hand. I doubt they have that at any state hospital. I've been thinking a lot about it, about how to make her comfortable until we can be together again.

I would do anything for her, even yoga. Early on, she did that thing most couples do, where she tried to drag me into it. She used to talk about it nonstop, the way people do when they love a thing, as though she felt that if she just hammered it enough, something would stick. So by osmosis, or her mouth, I learned more than enough about the practice. Oneness, in yogic philosophy, means unity, non-separation: me and you, us and nature, all of us. There's a science to it too—quantum physics demonstrates that what we thought were separate particles are actually connected waves of energy with no beginning and no end.

When I write this out, the doctor asks, "Are you trying to justify murder with physics?"

Stranger things have happened.

He comes every day now, although I'm only allotted three sessions a week. I don't know if he knows that I know this, or exactly what it is he wants. It's important to find out a person's motivations, but I'm in no hurry. Today, he looks at me with interest, but there's something else in his expression. Something I can't quite explain. Today I throw him a bone. I get to the point rather quickly, the way he prefers. *What do you know about quantum entanglement?*

"Quantum entanglement is the physical phenomenon that occurs when a pair or group of particles is generated, interact, or share spatial proximity in a way that the quantum state of each particle of the pair or group cannot be described independently of the state of the others, including when the particles are separated by a large distance...isn't that right?"

Exactly.

"You used to ask your victims questions before you killed them."

Liam did that.

"Right, Liam. Is that who is writing to me now?"

He set my house on fire and shot me in the face. It had better not be.

"You wrote that Liam was after fame."

I mean, I just assumed.

He cocks his head. "What is George after? What would you want to leave your fans with when you're gone—what would you want them to say about you?"

I think about this, but not for long. The other day I received a letter from Leslie. It contained a photograph of her growing belly. Supposedly. Truth is, it could be anyone's stomach. It could be anyone's baby. Leslie is exactly the kind of woman to pull that kind of stunt, the kind of woman who enjoys messing with you. The kind of woman who will make you go crazy. Like most things, only time will tell. About the baby, I mean. How ironic would it be? To have gotten everything you wanted, too late.

"George?"

He wants me to answer the question.

"What do you want to leave your fans with when you're gone?" This time he smiles and he waits. It makes me think of Liam. He doesn't know what I know: This is only temporary. Liam won't stay away forever. He's not that kind of guy. He'll resurface and I'll be out soon enough.

"What would you want them to say about you?"

195

Finally, I type the answer to his question. *Everything looks different in hindsight.*

"Anything else?"

They all went mad.

A NOTE FROM BRITNEY

Dear Reader,

I hope you enjoyed reading *The Book Doctor.*

Writing a book is an interesting adventure, it's a bit like inviting people into your brain to rummage around. *Look where my imagination took me. These are the kind of stories I like...*

That feeling is often intense and unforgettable. And mostly, a ton of fun.

With that in mind—thank you again for reading my work. I don't have the backing or the advertising dollars of big publishing, but hopefully I have something better...readers who like the same kind of stories I do. If you are one of them, please share with your friends and consider helping out by doing one (or all) of these quick things:

1. Visit my review page and write a 30 second review (even short ones make a big difference).

(http://britneyking.com/aint-too-proud-to-beg-for-reviews/)

Many readers don't realize what a difference reviews make but they make ALL the difference.

2. Drop me an email and let me know you left a review. This way I can enter you into my monthly drawing for signed paperback copies.

(hello@britneyking.com)

3. Point your psychological thriller loving friends to their free copies of my work. My favorite friends are those who introduce me to books I might like. **(http://www.britneyking.com)**

4. If you'd like to make sure you don't miss anything, to receive an email whenever I release a new title, sign up for my new release newsletter. **(https://britneyking.com/new-release-alerts/)**

Thanks for helping, and for reading my work. It means a lot.

Britney King

Austin, Texas

June 2020

ABOUT THE AUTHOR

Britney King lives in Austin, Texas with her husband, children, a dog named Gatsby, one ridiculous cat, and a partridge in a peach tree.

When she's not wrangling the things mentioned above, she writes psychological, domestic and romantic thrillers set in suburbia.

Without a doubt, she thinks connecting with readers is the best part of this gig. You can find Britney online here:

Email: britney@britneyking.com
Web: https://britneyking.com
Facebook: https://www.facebook.com/BritneyKingAuthor
Instagram: https://www.instagram.com/britneyking_/
Twitter: https://twitter.com/BritneyKing_
Goodreads: https://bit.ly/BritneyKingGoodreads
Pinterest: https://www.pinterest.com/britneyking_/

Happy reading.

ACKNOWLEDGMENTS

Many thanks to my family and friends for your support in my creative endeavors.

To the beta team, ARC team, and the bloggers, thank you for making this gig so much fun.

Last, but not least, thank you for reading my work. Thanks for making this dream of mine come true.

I appreciate you.

ALSO BY BRITNEY KING

Kill, Sleep, Repeat

An intense and deadly provocative thriller which follows a woman who, in a fight for survival, realizes her job may cost more than it pays.

Room 553

Room 553 is a standalone psychological thriller. Vivid and sensual, Room 553 weaves a story of cruelty, reckless lust, and blind, bloody justice.

HER

HER is a standalone psychological thriller which covers the dark side of female relationships. But equally—it's about every relationship anyone has ever had they knew was terrible for them. It's for those of us who swam for the deep end anyway, treading water because it seemed like more fun than sitting on the sidelines. It's about the lessons learned along the way. And knowing better the next time. Or not.

The Social Affair | Book One
The Replacement Wife | Book Two
Speak of the Devil | Book Three
The New Hope Series Box Set

The New Hope Series offers gripping, twisted, furiously clever reads that demand your attention, and keep you guessing until the very end. For fans of the anti-heroine and stories told in unorthodox ways, *The New Hope Series* delivers us the perfect dark and provocative villain. The only question—who is it?

Water Under The Bridge | Book One

Dead In The Water | Book Two

Come Hell or High Water | Book Three

The Water Series Box Set

The Water Trilogy follows the shady love story of unconventional married couple—he's an assassin—she kills for fun. It has been compared to a crazier book version of Mr. and Mrs. Smith. Also, Dexter.

Bedrock | Book One

Breaking Bedrock | Book Two

Beyond Bedrock | Book Three

The Bedrock Series Box Set

The Bedrock Series features an unlikely heroine who should have known better. Turns out, she didn't. Thus she finds herself tangled in a messy, dangerous, forbidden love story and face-to-face with a madman hell-bent on revenge. The series has been compared to Fatal Attraction, Single White Female, and Basic Instinct.

Around The Bend

Around The Bend, is a heart-pounding standalone which traces the journey of a well-to-do suburban housewife, and her life as it unravels, thanks to the secrets she keeps. If she were the only one with things she wanted to keep hidden, then maybe it wouldn't have turned out so bad. But she wasn't.

Somewhere With You | Book One

Anywhere With You | Book Two

The With You Series Box Set

The With You Series at its core is a deep love story about unlikely friends who travel the world; trying to find themselves, together and apart.

Packed with drama and adventure along with a heavy dose of suspense, it has been compared to The Secret Life of Walter Mitty and Love, Rosie.

SNEAK PEEK: THE SOCIAL AFFAIR

BOOK ONE

In the tradition of *Gone Girl* and *Behind Closed Doors* comes a gripping, twisted, furiously clever read that demands your attention, and keeps you guessing until the very end. For fans of the anti-heroine and stories told in unorthodox ways, *The Social Affair* delivers us the perfect dark and provocative villain. The only question—who is it?

A timeless, perfect couple waltzes into the small coffee shop where Izzy Lewis works. Instantly enamored, she does what she always does in situations like these: she searches them out on social media.

Just like that—with the tap of a screen— she's given a front row seat to the Dunns' picturesque life. This time, she's certain she's found what she's been searching for. This time, she'll go to whatever lengths it takes to ensure she gets it right—even if this means doing the unthinkable.

Intense and original, The Social Affair is a disturbing psychological thriller that explores what can happen when privacy is traded for convenience.

What readers are saying:

"Another amazingly well-written novel by Britney King. It's every bit as dark, twisted and mind twisting as Water Under The Bridge...maybe even a little more so."

"Hands down- best book by Britney King. Yet. She has delivered a difficult writing style so perfectly and effortlessly, that you just want to worship the book for the writing. The author has managed to make murder/assassination/accidental- gunshot- to-the-head- look easy. Necessary."

"Having fallen completely head over heels for these characters and this author with the first book in the series, I've been pretty much salivating over the thought of this book for months now. You'll be glad to know that it did not disappoint!"

Praise

"If Tarantino were a woman and wrote novels... they might read a bit like this."

"Fans of Gillian Flynn and Paula Hawkins meet your next obsession."

"Provocative and scary."

"A dark and edgy page-turner. What every good thriller is made of."

"I devoured this novel in a single sitting, absolutely enthralled by the storyline. The suspense was clever and unrelenting!"

"Completely original and complex."

"Compulsive and fun."

"No-holds-barred villains. Fine storytelling full of mystery and suspense."

"Fresh and breathtaking insight into the darkest corners of the human psyche."

THE SOCIAL AFFAIR

BRITNEY KING

COPYRIGHT

Hot Banana Press

Cover Design by Britney King LLC

Cover Image by Mario Azzi

Copy Editing by Librum Artis Editorial Services

Proofread by Proofreading by the Page

First Edition: 2018

ISBN 13: 978-1979057455

ISBN 10: 1979057451

britneyking.com

To those who've walked into our lives without first asking permission...

PROLOGUE

Attachment is an awfully hard thing to break. I should know. I surface from the depths of sleep to complete and utter darkness. I don't want to open my eyes. I have to. "I warned you, and I warned you," I hear his voice say. It's not the first time. He called out to me, speaking from the edge of consciousness, back when I thought this all might have been a dream. It's too late for wishful thinking now. This is his angry voice, the one I best try to avoid. My mind places it immediately. This one is reserved for special occasions, the worst of times.

I hear water running in the background. Or at least I think I do. For my sake, I hope I'm wrong. I try to recall what I was doing before, but this isn't that kind of sleep. It's the heavy kind, the kind you wake from and hardly know what year you're in, much less anything else. I consider how much time might have passed since I dozed off. Then it hits me.

"You really shouldn't have done that," he says, and his eyes come into focus. Those eyes, there's so much history in them; it's all still there now. I see it reflected back to me. I read a quote once that said... a true mark of maturity is when someone hurts you, and you try to understand their situation instead of trying to hurt them back. This seems idealistic now. I wish someone had warned me. Enough of that kind of thinking will get you killed.

"Please," I murmur, but the rest of what I want to say won't come. It's probably better this way. I glance toward the door, thinking about what's at stake if I don't make it out of here alive, wondering whether or not I can make a break for it. It's so dark out—a clear night, a moonless sky. The power is out, I gather, and it's a fair assumption. This has always been one of his favorite ways to show me what true suffering is like. That alone would make an escape difficult. I would have to set out on foot and then where would I go? Who would believe me?

"You have it too easy," he says, as though he wants to confirm my suspicions. "That's the problem nowadays. People consume everything, appreciate nothing."

He lifts me by the hair and drags me across the bedroom. I don't have to ask why. He doesn't like to argue where he sleeps, where we make love. It's one of our safe spaces, but like many things, this too is a facade. Nothing with him is safe.

"You like your comforts, but you forget nothing good comes without sacrifice."

"I haven't forgotten," I assure him, and that much is true. Sacrifice is something I know well.

He shakes his head, careful to exaggerate his movements. He wants the message he sends to sink in. "I don't know why you have to make me so angry."

I glance toward the window, thinking I see headlights, but it's wishful thinking. Then I reach up and touch the wet spot at the crown of my head. I pull my hand away, regretful I felt the need for confirmation. Instinct is enough. If only I'd realized this sooner. I didn't have to put my fingers to it to know there would be blood; the coppery scent fills the air. "It's not too bad," he huffs as he slides one hand under my armpit and hauls me up. "Come on," he presses, his fingertips digging into my skin. "Let's get you stitched up."

I follow his lead. There isn't another option. Head wounds bleed a lot, and someone's going to have to clean his mess up. If I live, that someone will be me. *This is how you stop the bleeding.* "What time is it?"

"Oh," he says, half-chuckling. "There's no need to worry about that. She's already come and gone."

I don't ask who he's referring to. I know. Everything in me sinks to the pit of my stomach. It rests there and I let it. I don't want him to see how deeply I am affected by what he's done. It's more dangerous if I let it show. But what I want to happen and what actually does, are two very different things. I know because my body tenses, as it gives over to emotion until eventually it seizes up completely. I don't mean for it to happen. It has a habit of betraying me, particularly where he is concerned. Your mind may know when something's bad for you. But the body can take a little longer. He knows where to touch me. He knows what to say. Automatic response is powerful, and like I said before, attachment is hard to break.

He shoves me hard into the wall. I guess I wasn't listening. I shouldn't have made a habit of that either. I don't feel the pain. I don't feel anything. "Ah, now look what you made me do," he huffs, running his fingers through his hair. He's staring at me as though this is the first time he's seeing me. His face is twisted. He wants me to think he's trying to work out his next move. He isn't. He's a planner, through and through.

Still, he's good at concealing what he doesn't want anyone to know. If only I'd been more like that. I wasn't. That's why I don't know if this is it, if this is the end. I only know where it began.

"We had an agreement," he reminds me. And he's right.

We did have an agreement.

That's how this all started.

READ MORE HERE: https://books2read.
com/b/thesocialaffair

Made in the USA
Monee, IL
13 December 2020

52635073R00135